"Please say you like to bake."

Sarah lifted one worried eyebrow in Renzo's direction.

"I do, actually."

"But you don't know how to bake anything? Like anything at all?" Kristi looked dumbfounded.

"Not even brownies in a box?" asked Naomi, setting four packs of marshmallow snowmen on the counter.

"I bet our mother could bake everything," muttered Chloe, just high enough to be heard. "I bet she liked doing things like that all the time."

Would her words deflate Sarah?

If they did, she didn't let it show. "Well, I can learn," Sarah assured her. "I'm pretty smart, and how hard can this be?"

Then she smiled. First at them. Then him. And when she did, it wasn't doom that wrought havoc in his chest.

He looked away, not because he wanted to, but because he had to, and that was a different situation altogether.

Multipublished bestselling author **Ruth Logan Herne** loves God, her country, her family, dogs, chocolate and coffee! Married to a very patient man, she lives in an old farmhouse in Upstate New York and thinks possums should leave the cat food alone and snakes should always live outside. There are no exceptions to either rule! Visit Ruth at ruthloganherne.com.

Visit the Author Profile page at Harlequin.com for more titles.

Finding Her Christmas Family

Ruth Logan Herne

LOVE INSPIRED
INSPIRATIONAL ROMANCE

LOVE INSPIRED®
INSPIRATIONAL ROMANCE

ISBN-13: 978-1-335-48844-2

Finding Her Christmas Family

Copyright © 2020 by Ruth M. Blodgett

This edition published by arrangement with Harlequin Books S.A.

For questions and comments about the quality of this book,
please contact us at CustomerService@Harlequin.com.

Love Inspired
22 Adelaide St. West, 40th Floor
Toronto, Ontario M5H 4E3, Canada
www.Harlequin.com

Printed in U.S.A.

And the child grew, and she brought him unto
Pharaoh's daughter, and he became her son.
And she called his name Moses: and she said,
Because I drew him out of the water.
—*Exodus* 2:10

This story is lovingly dedicated to all in my family who have been on either side of adoption. Michael (Stevie)…Kelly…Tendai Patricia…Ruth…and our beloved Nathan. Throughout all time, you are loved. Thank you for being the blessings you are.

Chapter One

Heat climbed Detective Lorenzo Calloway's collar as he approached the Golden Grove playground on a surprisingly gorgeous November day. He spotted his mother sitting on one of the many wooden benches surrounding the play area. Eyes down, her fingers flew, knitting something for the girls, most likely. And the triplets, three darlings his parents took in as newborns, were scrambling around the primary-color-schemed play area. Even Kristi, whose initial newborn prognosis had seemed dire, was now hale and hearty, thanks to modern medicine and his family's tireless devotion to these girls. Three beautiful look-alikes who had come into their lives when their mother died unexpectedly.

Suddenly—beyond the upper fence, on a slight incline—Lorenzo saw a woman, snapping pictures of them.

Suspicion didn't crawl up his spine. It raced. When families dealt with kids in foster care, a lot of things could go wrong, but the triplets' case was clear. Their maternal grandmother had passed away over a decade before, and their grandfather was struggling with a degenerative nerve illness. Jenn Drew had taken all of that into consideration when she'd asked his family to take care of the girls if anything ever happened to her. No one expected that would be the case.

And then it was.

You're overreacting. People take pictures of the girls all the time.

They did. The sight of identical triplets made folks pause and sometimes even squeal in delight; a weird way for the girls to grow up, in his opinion. But they couldn't isolate them, and it was a reaction they would probably deal with for a long time to come.

But to take shots of someone else's kids from a distance with what looked like a progressive lens wasn't normal. And because he was over the moon in love with these three little ones, his reaction might be a little over the top, too.

The tall, slim photographer hadn't noticed him. Since he'd caught sight of her, she hadn't taken her camera or her gaze off the girls, and that was enough to spike his protective instincts to a whole other level.

Renzo looped around the curving sidewalk toward Park Road, and when he got closer, he turned and made a beeline for the woman, across the grass, wishing he was in uniform. He wasn't, but he had no problem flashing his badge and letting her know that he didn't appreciate people taking liberty with the sweet orphans that had been entrusted to their family. They wouldn't be orphans for much longer, once his parents' adoption application was approved.

The grass muted his footfalls. He stopped directly behind her.

Click! Click! Click!

The auto-take on the pricey camera shot in rapid succession, and the camera never shifted when a couple of other kids raced onto the playground equipment. It stayed right there, aimed directly at Kristi, Chloe and Naomi. He folded his arms, braced his legs and cleared his throat loudly.

That got her attention.

She whirled around, surprised.

And then he was the one surprised. Looking back at him from an absolutely lovely face was the image of Jenn Drew, the girls' mother. Golden, wavy hair. Golden-brown eyes. Pale skin without a hint of freckle. Except Jenn had passed away over three years ago. He stared at her.

She stared right back, then set the camera on a leather satchel, straightened and faced him. "Is there a problem?"

Yes, there was a problem because there was no way the resemblance he saw could be coincidental. In fact, if he hadn't known Jenn so well, he'd have mistaken this woman for her. And how could that be?

Stop. Think like a cop.

"You're taking pictures of our girls. Without permission." He watched her eyes widen at the term "our girls." "Why?"

"*Your* girls?" She frowned without really frowning,

a neat trick, something Jenn had been able to do, too. "You're their father?"

A warning thrum climbed his spine. "You answered my question with a question. Clever, but it's not going to work. Why are you in the park taking pictures of them? It's a simple enough request."

Simple, yes. But there was nothing simple about her response.

"Because I am their Aunt Sarah." She faced him full-on, calm and cool. "Dr. Sarah Brown from Seattle Children's Hospital. Their mother, Jenn Drew, was my sister and I've come to claim what's mine."

Renzo's heart went tight. His palms grew damp, and he swiped them against the sides of his jeans. "Jenn had no sisters."

"No known sisters, I suppose." The incredibly beautiful woman kept her gaze on his. She seemed calm while he was the opposite of calm because the thought of the girls being wrenched away from his family was preposterous. They were on the verge of having the adoption finalized. "And while this was as much a surprise to me as it is to you, I can assure you that DNA evidence doesn't lie. At some point Jenn Drew submitted a DNA sample to a research company. This year, a group of my friends and I did the same thing. When I received my results, I discovered my closest relative, a full sister, was living two hours from me, and I never knew she existed."

"Why would your parents give away a child?" It made no sense to Renzo. Why give away one daughter and keep the other? Who would do something like that?

Her response cleared up that question. "Our biological mother put us up for adoption thirty-four years ago. Because of the high demand for infants, the adoption agency split us up. Neither family was made aware of the other girl's existence. I initiated an investigation as soon as I realized I had a sister, and soon found out that she was gone before I even had a chance to know her. To love her." She hoisted the slim folder from her satchel. "But now my goal is to regain control of our lives and our destinies, Mr....?"

He didn't extend his hand. If this was someone else's story, he'd be more compassionate, but it wasn't. He and his parents had raised the girls from birth. He needed to think, and not pretend an empathy he didn't have. "Detective Lorenzo Calloway. Grant County Sheriff's Department."

"Well, Detective Calloway." Her firm tone didn't give an inch of deference to his position or title. "While I'm sorry to surprise you with all of this—"

"Odd, you don't sound sorry," he mused purposely, watching for her reaction and when she gave it, she surprised him again.

"But I am." She kept her eyes on his, then indicated Kristi, Chloe and Naomi with a wave. "For thirty-four years Jenn and I had no knowledge of each other. It was a blessing that we both had good homes, but we didn't have the one thing we truly deserved. A chance to know one another. We were separated like a litter of puppies." She jutted her chin toward the girls. "I was robbed of the chance to know my sister. To love her. I intend to make sure that doesn't happen again."

Seeing this through her point of view didn't just spur his compassion. It magnified it. "I don't downplay the stupidity of an agency that did that. My family has provided foster care for over twenty years, and we've taken in several sibling groups. The thought of separating brothers and sisters is repugnant. Which is why Jenn's daughters are on the ranch, because my parents would have never let them be separated. And Jenn loved us."

Her face relaxed.

He didn't let the change of expression fool him, though. Being a cop taught him to avoid overspeak. When talking potential lawsuits, less was more. He nodded toward the playground. "You need to meet my mother. My father. And the girls."

"You think that having me come and see what a happy little family your parents have provided will change my goal." She aimed a pointed look at him. "I can assure you, it won't." She wasn't tall now that he was up close, but not petite, either. Probably five foot six, and wearing heels and a classy outfit that made her stand out in their small town of Golden Grove in Central Washington. Jenn had been easygoing and casual. A physician's assistant in nearby Wenatchee.

Despite the physical resemblance with Jenn, this woman was neither easygoing nor casual, and that made her seem more formidable. "Look." He folded his arms. She noted the gesture with one slightly arched brow "You're understandably upset."

That statement got his first full-on reaction. She rolled her eyes, impatient. "I get that. And I get that you probably have decades of anger issues that you'd like to unload on me right about now."

"I am not angry. I am determined."

"Right." He wasn't going to fight with her. He knew the value of time in police work. A good interrogation was never hurried, and the suspect should be made comfortable.

Initially, that is.

And then maybe not so comfortable as time went on.

He hoped that wouldn't be necessary. If what she said was true, she and Jenn had been dealt a raw deal over three decades ago, but he'd learned one firm lesson dealing with life and police work: life wasn't always fair. Sometimes the wrong things happened and you learned to live with it or let it pull you into the abyss.

He'd learned to sidestep the abyss a long time ago. "Come to the ranch tonight. I'll explain to my mother—"

"That woman is your mother?" She indicated his mother on the bench.

"Yes. And while she will welcome you because that's the kind of woman she is, I will be more careful in my assessment, Dr. Brown, because that's the kind of cop I am. And if you want to meet the girls, you'll do it on my terms. Or wait your turn in court."

Lorenzo had grown up fishing the creeks, rivers and reservoirs of the Columbian Plateau. Reeling in a big catch wasn't done quickly. It was teased in, bit by bit until the fish was too tired to resist. It was a ploy he used in police work on a regular basis.

There was nothing regular about this new development, but he knew his mother. She'd want to meet Dr. Sarah Brown and befriend her. And no matter how much he might advise against that, his mother would brush off his concerns and welcome the girls' new-found relative. Even if it meant she'd come to take the girls away.

His mother was blessed with a gentle heart.

Time and experience had hardened his, so when Sarah finally acquiesced with a slight nod, he began planning his next move: find out every detail he could about her. No one skated through life perfectly. Every-one had an Achilles' heel. His job would be to find hers and use it as needed.

He pulled out his phone. "Give me your number and I'll call so you've got me in your contact list."

She hesitated for a fraction of a second, as if unsure of his intentions, but wasn't this how everyone con-nected these days?

She reeled off the number. He sent her a quick text with his parents' address. "Six o'clock good?"

She'd turned back toward the girls and her expression had gone soft. It morphed into full professional mode when she redirected her attention to him. "That's fine."

"Then I'll see you in about two hours."

A flash of uncertainty told him she wasn't as invul-nerable as she liked to appear.

A weak spot.

Good.

He walked away. Yes, he was setting her up pur-posely and he was pretty sure she knew it. But it wasn't what your opponent knew. It was how they defended their position. It was—

He gave himself a mental smackdown.

This wasn't a case on his crime docket. This was family, three children who'd become part of the Calloways nearly four years before. Children they loved as their own, who could logistically be taken away with Sarah Brown's surprise appearance. Given her story, how could he prevent that from happening?

And worse…

Should he?

A cop.

And not just any cop. A detective. That meant he'd go full bore, checking her out.

Let him check. Sarah had absolutely nothing to hide.

She slipped her camera into the leather messenger pouch her parents had gifted her when she graduated from med school ten years ago. She hadn't wanted a typical bag, and they'd laughed because they knew her. Loved her. And they still loved her, even with her current quest to find out more about her displaced family.

They didn't know about this new twist, though. Her long-lost sister and three nieces. She'd kept that to herself purposely. Her parents would be furious to discover she had a sister who had been placed elsewhere. They'd noted way back when that they'd been open to a sibling group.

She'd tell them when she knew more. Right now she was on a fact-finding mission, the same kind of thing she did when figuring out the best way to handle the delicate interventions on premature babies. As a neonatologist, she faced joy and sorrow on a regular basis, but these days there were more successes in the NICU, and something about coaxing the tiniest babies into a state of wellness rejuvenated her.

She'd taken long-unused vacation time to find out whatever she could and set her plan for the girls in motion. No matter what, those children should be raised by one of their own. Someone from their family. And she was the only one who could do that. Her DNA search had turned up several probable cousins in the heartland, but no one closer. That meant she was it. She had the education and the means to provide for them, and the love. And she was their aunt, their next of kin, only no one had known that at the time.

They'd know it now.

The cop had gone around the park. He was approaching his mother.

Sarah didn't want their first contact to be over the expanse of green grass. She tucked her satchel over her arm and crossed to her white SUV, but peeked back as she opened the door. From this distance the seated woman shouldn't be able to see her.

But the son could.

She waved to him, a friendly gesture. Then climbed into her vehicle.

Let him ponder that, she decided. She drove to a coffee shop and bakery in Wenatchee, ordered a latte with an extra shot of much-needed espresso, and a beautiful layer cake to bring to the Calloway house.

Nerves made her hands shake.

Her hands never shook. They couldn't. She dealt with the tiniest of babies in the neonatal ward, but today, the thought of seeing her nieces unnerved her.

She sipped the coffee.

It burned her tongue. Her fault for ordering it extra hot, then sipping too soon.

She was hungry, but didn't dare eat. Stress always messed with her digestion and the cop unnerved her.

She could admit that now that she was on her own. He wasn't the kind of person a smart woman shrugged off, and not because of his ridiculous good looks. Yeah, she'd noticed the sky blue eyes, dark, wavy hair and thick eyebrows.

Dark Irish. Like her adoptive grandmother, Grace Harrigan.

She puffed a cooling breath over the top of her latte and wanted to cry.

Sarah Brown never cried. She stared at the coffee and the pretty boxed cake and fought back tears. Then she did what she probably should have done weeks before.

She called her mother. Lindsay Brown might not look like her, with her short dark hair and big brown eyes, but she loved her. So why was she trying to do this on her own?

Stupidly independent.

An old boyfriend had used that phrase as he walked out on her over two years before.

She didn't hate him because he left. She'd hated that he was right and that she couldn't seem to forge a real relationship with anyone.

When her mother answered the phone, Sarah spilled it all and cried the whole time she did.

"I'm on my way."

Sarah had taken an outdoor patio table at the café, facing outward so no one would notice her or hear her. "Mom, no…"

"Yes," her mother replied. "Sarah, you have lived your life with such strength, and I don't doubt you can handle anything that comes your way, but you weren't the only person wronged by that agency. I am beyond furious and while your dad has to stay here, I am retired. Give me the name of your hotel, and I'll book a room and be on my way in twenty minutes. Do you want to put off your meeting with them tonight?"

"No." She swabbed her eyes and blew her nose. Both gestures helped her regain control. "I'll meet with them, and I'll be strong because I know you'll be waiting when I get back. And it's not a hotel. I rented a temporary apartment."

"Text me the address and I'll put it in my GPS."

"I will. And Mom?"

"Yes, honey?"

"Thank you."

"Oh, darling. No thanks needed. We've got this."

She hung up the phone and went back to the apartment to freshen up, and then, at quarter to six, she put the cake and her bag in the car and followed the directions to the Calloways' home. When she crested a hill, an expanse of black and red cattle splayed out before her. Loud, raucous cattle, bleating and bawling, just beyond a sign that read Welcome to Calloway Ranch. She turned into the drive.

Nothing in her life had prepared her for the mass of crying cows on one side of the road and what looked like a huge herd of others on the opposite side, two fences up.

Hundreds of cows, calling to one another.

And every one of them looked desperately unhappy. What kind of place was this?

Chapter Two

"I didn't know you were separating the cows from the calves today." Renzo glanced at the clock, then his dad, and then through the window at the gravel drive running beneath the big Calloway Ranch sign. No one liked the annual task of separating cows from their big, burly calves, but it had to be done. Had he known his dad and brother were doing it today, he wouldn't have asked Sarah Brown to come to the house. Even at this distance, the mournful bellows cast a pall over just about everything for three days, until the cows wandered off in resignation.

"I meant to do it last week, but there wasn't enough manpower," Roy Calloway explained. "I had your brother here today, and we borrowed a hand from Powell's farm, but that last group gave me and Kyle a hard time."

Kyle was Renzo's younger brother. He worked the ranch with their father, and lived up the road with his wife Valerie.

His father poured a mug of fresh coffee from the old-style pot he loved and took a seat. "I'm just glad it's done before the weather turns." Then he seemed to notice Renzo's expression. "Why the concern about dividing the herd today?"

Separating the calves was an annual ritual before they were sent off to market. On sale day his parents treated workers to dinner at a nearby steakhouse, their way of saying thank you for another good year. Renzo jutted his chin toward the driveway. "The girls' aunt is coming here, and the bawling cows are going to set a really interesting stage for someone given away as a baby," he explained.

"The girls' aunt?" Roy frowned.

He looked tired tonight. More so than usual, and Renzo wished his father had asked for help. He'd never minded helping out, but his father liked to prove he had everything under control, which was generally true. But maybe not so true today.

"They've got no aunt, Renzo."

"It seems they do." He explained the situation to his father while his mother finished bathing the girls. He'd just completed an abbreviated version of the story when Chloe slid down the slick oak bannister and plopped onto the floor with a gymnast's flair. "Ta-da!" She threw her hands into a winner's pose, then dashed toward Renzo. "I have three things to say to you, mister."

Chloe held nothing back, ever. Her personality didn't just collide with her calmer sisters, it ricocheted. He swept her up and met her eye to eye. "And what would those be?"

"I 'spected you to read me a story last night and then I didn't see a speck of you."

"Because I was working, and I do believe I explained that before I went to work yesterday afternoon."

"'Cept that I was thinking you would sneak over here and read to me anyway," she went on as if it was perfectly fine for him to duck out of work and read stories to little girls.

"My boss would take exception to that, honeybunch."

"Well, me too," she insisted. "I took a lot of 'ception to that because I 'spected you and you didn't come even though I looked and looked out the window for you. And the cows are noisy."

"Is that it?"

"What?"

He laughed at her, snuggling her close. "Is that all you've got to say to me?" he added, because Chloe always had something else to say.

Her voice hiked up. "Who's that?"

His chest squeezed tight as he turned to see the faint cloud of gravel dust kicked up by Sarah Brown's white SUV. What should he say to Chloe?

The truth, he decided. "There's a friend coming to meet you girls."

"All of us?" came another voice. A different voice, which always struck him by surprise whenever Naomi spoke. Winsome as ever, Naomi didn't slide down the bannister. She walked down the stairs like the princess she longed to be, and her neatly plaited hair was a silent testimony to their differences. Chloe had "wild child" written in her DNA.

Not Naomi. She was an anxious-to-please child, with a giving nature. A born peacemaker. She skipped across the living room and opened the door. "Should we turn the lights on?"

"Sure." The dusk-to-dawn barnyard lights flickered on just then, a reminder of shorter days and longer nights as fall marched toward winter. He saw the movement of the car door once Sarah parked the SUV, and then Naomi put her little hand to her chest. "Oh, she's pretty!"

"Let me see!" Not to be outdone, Chloe dashed across the room, slid across the tile entry and came to a hard stop as she crashed into the wall. "Nomi. You didn't give me enough room to land and so I banged my head and it's all your fault." She stomped her foot, never a good sign. Renzo moved between the two quickly. Naomi might be the quieter one, but she didn't take a lot of her sister's flak.

"I didn't move," she protested. "I stayed right here. You just—" She paused as Sarah Brown approached. Her mouth dropped open. And when Chloe whirled around, hers did the same.

A woman who looked very much like the picture of their mother on the living room wall stood before them.

He expected Naomi to hang back, but she pulled the door open wider and it was the boisterous Chloe who seemed dumbstruck by Sarah's arrival. When she came in, carrying a delicious-looking cake, Renzo went down on one knee between the two girls and said words that came mighty hard. "Girls, this is your Aunt Sarah. Your mommy's sister."

"Our mom had a sister?" Naomi's tone filled with wonder and doubt. "I don't think our mom did, Renzo. But maybe…" She gulped hard as she struggled to make sense of this new twist. Then she looked from Sarah to Jenn's photograph and back, confused. "This is our mom, for real?"

"Our mom isn't for real, Nomi." Chloe went back to instant overreaction mode. "She's in heaven, and you can't come back from there. Like ever. Mama Gina told us that and I believe everything Mama Gina says."

"That's kept me out of no small number of tight spots myself," Roy Calloway spouted as he came around the corner. He indicated his dirty work clothes with a grimace and the wailing cows with both hands. "I didn't know we were expecting company, or I'd have cleaned up quicker, but muck's a part of ranch life. How do you do, ma'am." He extended his hand with the finesse of a diplomat. "Welcome to our home. And it's a pleasure to know that the girls have such lovely family after all this time."

Sarah's eyes narrowed. She glanced at his hand, and Renzo was pretty sure she was debating whether to take it, then she did. Lightly. Briefly. With the barest of touches, and that annoyed him, but at least she did it. "It's a pleasure to meet you."

"I'm ready for a cleanup if my gals are out of the upstairs bath?" He palmed Naomi's head, then Chloe's. "You two look clean to me, and smell good enough to eat up."

They giggled and hugged him as Renzo took the cake box from Sarah's hands and set it on a nearby table.

"You can't eat us, Papa!" Naomi tipped back her head and laughed up at him. "We're not hot dogs, you know!"

"More like birds, that's for certain."

Chloe pretended her arms were wings. "Bawk! Bawk! Bawwwwwk! Can't catch me, Papa!"

The race was on.

She dodged right, his father darted left, and within five seconds both girls were racing around the room, squealing with joy.

And then his father collapsed.

Like a slow-motion movie, his father's happy, laughing face contorted. The smile became a contortion.

His hand came up, toward his chest. His mouth opened, as if to say something, but no sound came out.

The other hand reached for the sofa, but missed and Roy didn't slip to the floor.

He crashed.

"Dad!" Renzo was by his side in a heartbeat.

Bright blue eyes stared up at him. Then he blinked, real slow. He opened his mouth again.

But only part of his mouth opened. The right side was at an awkward angle and his right eye drooped.

Stroke.

Then his father's eyes closed. His breathing paused… and didn't restart. When Renzo put his ear to Roy's chest, there was no comforting sound of the heartbeat that had worked so diligently for over sixty years to help build Calloway Ranch.

Don't think, man. React. You know what to do. You're trained.

Renzo started to rearrange his father's body for CPR,

but someone beat him to it. The sofa table that the girls had dodged around was shoved back, out of the way, and Sarah Brown dropped to her knees alongside his father. She'd yanked a stethoscope from what he'd thought was just a camera bag and applied it to his father's chest, then barked orders. "Is he on any meds?"

"No."

"Get me aspirin ASAP, call 911, get medics here pronto, tell them cardio resuscitation is needed."

Before he had his cell phone in his hand, she was doing chest compressions. Under her breath she hummed the tune of one of the girls' favorite songs. The movement of her hands synchronized with the rhythm of the tune.

"Mom! I need you ASAP!" he hollered up the stairs, grabbed an aspirin bottle from above the refrigerator, and called Dispatch while handing Sarah the aspirin. Within seconds he realized there was no way his father could chew or swallow the aspirin in his current condition.

Sarah seemed to realize that, too. She shook her head and kept up the compressions.

Chloe and Naomi had shrunk back with matching looks of fright and tears streaming, but he couldn't help that now as he guided them into the wide-open back room.

The 911 center call went through. "We need a bus for 4217 Old North Road," he barked into the phone. "Male, age sixty-six, Caucasian, cardio resuscitation needed, stroke symptoms noted."

"Renzo, it's Clem, we'll get right out there. Are you alone with Roy?"

Renzo heard Clem key the call into the county-wide service as he answered. "No, Mom's here, I've got the girls and a visiting doctor but he's not good, Clem."

"We know the way, Renzo. Sit tight."

His mother came down the stairs, carrying Kristi. As she approached the bottom of the stairs, realization hit. "Renzo, what's happened? Roy?" She set Kristi down and rushed to her husband's side. "Roy, it's Gina. Hang on, darling, hang on, okay? Help's coming!" Then she looked up to Renzo for reassurance and he gave a quick, firm nod as he reached out for all three girls.

"Ambulance is on its way. Hey, gals, how about you come into the family room with me, okay?" He drew the girls into the room that overlooked acres of pastures backdropped by the rugged frames of the highlands separating the Cascade Range from the Rocky Mountains to the east.

There was nothing to see in the darkness. Nothing to distract three little beauties from the life-and-death struggle in the adjoining room and the ceaseless bawling of sorrowed cows on all sides of the house. Under normal circumstances he'd amuse them by playing a game.

Nothing was normal right now.

His father was gravely ill and a relative of the triplets, probably intent on taking them away, was trying to save Roy Calloway's life.

He prayed she'd succeed.

He wasn't sure what to pray next, but he knew he

needed to calm the girls' fears, and the best way he knew to do that was to pray. Not for them. With them.

Sarah applied her hands to the aging rancher's chest in a well-spaced rhythm that matched a human heartbeat and a couple of popular songs. A kid's song had come to mind today.

Maybe it was being surrounded by three look-alikes that reminded her so much of herself. And the look on the faces of the two she'd met, Chloe and Naomi.

Beautiful. Funny. Pesky. Endearing.

Three girls, all related to her, the offspring of the sister she never knew.

She wanted them.

She'd known that from the time she discovered their existence. Her sister's obituary listed an aging father, a deceased mother, several cousins, aunts and uncles and three infant daughters who were now nearly four years old.

These girls were her family.

She was theirs. And nobody was going to stand in her way, but as she continued the chest compressions, she couldn't erase the image of Chloe's face.

Or was it Naomi's?

In the hustle of moving furniture to gain access to the detective's father, she wasn't sure.

As the wail of a siren grew louder and Gina Calloway's voice crooned words of love and encouragement to her critically ill husband, she needed to think of one thing and one thing only. To focus on keeping her rhythm smooth and her hands moving despite the current ache in her shoulders.

His eyelids flickered slightly.

Gina gushed a thankful prayer for the movement and for Sarah's presence.

She wouldn't be thanking her soon. Gina Calloway would probably hate her, and so would the rest of the family. She was trying to save Roy's life only to take a big chunk of it away.

Irony at its worst because her goal was to salvage what little biological family she had.

Roy didn't know her intent. Neither did Gina.

She did. Somewhere a door banged shut. Then a movement shifted a shadow between the hall light and this room. She looked up.

The detective stood there, watching her. Watching his father. Seeing his mother gripping his father's right hand, her lips moving in silent prayer.

He knew why she was here.

She saw it in his stance. His gaze. The strong set of his shoulders.

He was watching her save a man's life before she destroyed it.

He moved forward and came down by her side, opposite his mother. "Want me to sub in?"

The wail of the siren intensified. Help was close at hand. "No, I'm good. Can you get the door and guide them in? Who's got the girls?"

"My brother just got here. He lives up the road." He hurried to the door while she continued the downward thrusts in a rhythmic beat, and when she was pretty sure she couldn't take much more, the EMT slipped into place beside her.

"We've got this, ma'am."

She moved over to give him room and as they ran an assessment, she heard the conversation over their shoulder radios.

Lorenzo drew his mother in for a hug.

He was a protector. A guardian. The dog at the gate, watching for wolves, and she'd come into Central Washington as a wolf in designer clothing.

His gaze met hers as the medics worked to get Roy stable enough for transport, and she read concern, love and fear in his eyes.

She shifted her attention to the first responders. "Where's the nearest Level One stroke center?" she asked. "Let's get him there ASAP."

"No Level Ones within three hours, ma'am. We've got a Level Two in Wenatchee."

Her mouth dropped open. "Three hours?"

"More, actually."

There was no way this man should be in transport for an extended period of time, but the reality of being three hours away from the best care shocked her. She'd been raised near first-class medicine all her life, so the thought of having it unavailable seemed absurd. "Let's get him to Wenatchee. If he stabilizes, he should be moved to Level One."

"You mean if he lives."

Mrs. Calloway's voice cut right to the chase. Sarah nodded. "He's in serious danger, I'm afraid."

The medics had cinched Roy in. They began trundling the gurney.

Gina left Lorenzo's side and grabbed one of Sarah's hands in a fleeting touch. "God put you in our living room at just the right time, Sarah Brown, and you've given him a chance. What more can I ask?" Then she hurried away after the medics.

Another man appeared. He looked like a blonder version of Lorenzo and had those same blue eyes. Their father's eyes. "I'll take Mom. You're okay here?"

"Yes. I'll watch the girls."

"They're scared." He hadn't looked her way. Then he did.

His face went pale. Sarah saved him by speaking up.

"I'm Sarah Brown, a doctor from Seattle, and Jenn was my sister."

He seemed to accept her minimized explanation as he rushed out the door. The mass exodus of people and equipment left a gap. The cozy front room felt suddenly empty. Lorenzo crossed the braided carpet and turned to her. "Thank you."

She started to speak, but he raised a hand. "Whatever happens, whatever is planned, it's all for another day, Sarah. Tonight is all about him." He indicated the ambulance with a thrust of his chin. "And them. So let's give those beautiful children a semblance of normal. Okay?"

When he said her name in that slightly Western tone, the timbre of his voice made it sound special. All her life she'd been special. She knew that. Smart. Focused. Wise beyond her years, with an affinity for learning that set her apart.

But she hadn't come here in peace, and that reality cut deep right now.

"Come back to the family room. Let's have you meet the girls properly. Our only job tonight, yours and mine, is to get their minds on something else, but they love my dad, so it won't be easy."

She followed him to the back of the house where a broad, bright kitchen flowed into a living and dining area, flooded with light.

Three little girls huddled together on a biscuit-colored leather sofa. Three tear-streaked faces stared up at them as they entered the room. Then one girl wearing lime-green pajamas rushed forward, hurling herself into the detective's arms. "I promised Kyle I'd be brave," she whispered. "But I'm not even a little brave, Renzo. And I don't want to be."

He sank to the floor, and the other girls raced to pile on him.

They love him.

And he clearly loved them. The image of him on the floor, surrounded by three beautiful girls amazed her, and for just a moment it seemed right. So right.

Then reality swept in.

She'd been loved, too. All her life. But she'd also been separated from her only sister, and she'd never had the chance to meet her.

It was clear that Chloe, Kristi and Naomi loved this family and her goal wasn't to break their hearts, but to establish family roots for them to reach out and excel.

She'd lived a good life. This wasn't about adoption. Being adopted had been a blessing to her.

But a complete stranger had changed two children's lives irreparably.

She would never see Jenn. Talk to her. Get to know her. Laugh with her. Argue with her. Love her.

Her precious nieces wouldn't have to face a lifetime of wondering who they were. Who they might be related to. Or even who they resembled, because somehow their aunt was going to be part of their lives from this moment on.

Chapter Three

Renzo realized that the incredibly beautiful and smart Sarah Brown had come to Golden Grove to turn their lives upside down.

But the good Lord had beat her to it.

In the meantime, Renzo was in charge and the three little girls he'd helped raise needed him.

He'd dropped to the floor like he often did at story time.

Would Sarah join him there?

She didn't. She took a seat on the edge of the lounger as if she wanted to complete their circle, but couldn't quite do it.

The girls instantly snuggled into him, only this time was different. This wasn't the time to jump right into funny books about a mischievous kindergartener or the nonsensical rhymes they loved so well. Tonight it was God, first. "Let's start with a prayer for Papa. Okay?"

Three worried heads nodded. They all clasped hands, then Naomi seemed to realize they'd left Sarah out, so she reached up and clasped her aunt's hand, then jutted her chin toward Kristi. "Now you can hold her hand, and we're a big circle. Okay?"

Naomi's gesture startled her aunt. The surprise softened her affect. She took Naomi's hand, then Kristi's, then turned his way. The fact that it seemed right smacked him upside the head. Was it because she looked so much like Jenn? Or because she matched the girls in appearance and he didn't?

That was a conversation for a different time. He squeezed Naomi's hand lightly, then Chloe's. And then he prayed. He kept the words simple. "Dear God, we ask you to bless Papa. To give his heart and his head strength and healing."

He opened his eyes.

Three faces gazed up at him. Three faces filled with fear and worry, and he was pretty sure his wasn't much better.

"We thank you for Aunt Sarah's help, for putting her in exactly the right place at the right time, and for the grace of healing hands on our doorstep."

It was a good prayer. But it was overwhelmed by the continual bawling and bleating of the angry cows on two sides of the house, and there was nothing he could do about that.

"Will Papa die?"

Kristi uttered what all three girls were probably thinking. He started to shake his head, but he'd promised them honesty from the time they were babies. That meant he couldn't shade the truth now. "I don't know, Kristi. I hope not because I don't want him to. We don't know what God's got planned. So we'll pray for him to heal, okay?"

She nodded. So did Naomi.

Not Chloe. She let go of his hand, folded her arms in a really tight clench and shrieked, "I don't want him to die! Why does everything always have to go so bad in this dumb world?"

He hauled her in closer. "Hey, it's okay to be angry, but not to scream, all right? Papa can't have people screaming right now, so let's practice our inside voices for when he comes back home."

"There shouldn't ever be screaming," scolded Naomi. "I think we should all be so very nice and pray that way, too. And not yell about every little thing."

Kristi didn't buy into Naomi's polite reasoning. She put a protective arm around Chloe. "Well, I want to scream, too. Ever since I hit my head in the bathtub upstairs when I was climbing out, all I wanted to do was scream and now Papa's sick and my head doesn't even really hurt anymore but I still want to scream. Only I won't."

"I'm sorry you hit your head, darling." Renzo leaned down and kissed the side of her forehead. He hadn't noticed the small bump before. "I'm sorry for all of this. But sometimes things don't go our way and God wants us to do our best to be big and brave and bold."

"Well, I'm almost *this* many." Kristi held up four fingers. "And I'm not big, but I am very brave and very bold. I think."

"You are." He smiled down at her, the baby who'd been hospitalized much longer than her sisters. "You hung on through some tough times when you were tiny, and we knew you were a born fighter, Tough Stuff."

The nickname made her grin and she flexed her biceps to demonstrate just how fierce she was.

"Why did Mama Gina have to go, too?" demanded Chloe. "Who will put us to bed? And take us to pre-k? And make us food? And wash stuff?"

Renzo sent her a look of exaggerated surprise. "Um, duh. Me, of course."

He made a face that had them giggling for just a moment, then when they remembered what had happened, they stopped.

"I'll be here," he assured them. "I'll take some vacation time I've been storing up, and we'll take care of things together. Three big girls like you and a big guy like me, we've got all we need to handle things around here. You help me and I'll help you. Now, I want you to *really* meet your Aunt Sarah." He motioned toward her. "She came a long way to see you. She's very excited to get to know you, but she got a little busy helping Papa."

"You maybe saved his life," noted Chloe, not all that softly because the girl rarely did anything quietly. "I heard Mama Gina say that, and I can't even believe that I have such a beautiful auntie and you save lives and my friend Nathan will be so surprised because he doesn't have an aunt *or* an uncle," she explained in her typical quick-speak way. "Renzo pretends to be his uncle, but he's not for real, and Nathan will be so surprised that I have one. He won't even really believe it, maybe. So I'll have to show him, okay?"

Sarah had been watching their back and forth quietly. Now she sank to the carpeted floor, between the girls. Coming down to their level didn't just make her seem less formidable. It made her fit in. Beautifully. Perfectly. As if she was made to be part of their family because she was part of their family. Unfortunately, there was the tiny problem of custody.

Would Sarah launch her quest after seeing the close-knit family they'd become?

Sarah offered Chloe a gentle smile. "I will enjoy meeting your friend, Chloe. But not as much as I enjoy meeting my three nieces. Three beautiful girls who remind me of myself when I was a little girl."

"We have hair like you. Like the same color, almost," noted Kristi. "And like our mom," she finished matter-of-factly.

"And brownish eyes," explained Naomi. "Kind of greeny-brown," she added. "I think it's weird to all have the same eyes, don't you?" She reached out to touch Sarah's pants. She seemed intrigued by the smoothness of the silky weave. "But Mama Gina has dark brown eyes and Renzo and Papa and Kyle have blue eyes, and Mama Gina says that way the girls win because we have more brown eyes than blue ones but old Callie-cat has yellow eyes, and no one else in the family has yellow eyes, so she's never going to win. Do your mom and dad have brown eyes? Or blue ones? And do you have a cat or a dog or like anything?" Naomi posed the question with a mix of childlike innocence and the instincts of an investigative reporter.

Renzo waited for Sarah to answer. And when she

did, she didn't disappoint them, which somehow made the horrific evening a little bit better.

"One cat at my parents' house," Sarah explained. "And one kind of spoiled dog. I always said that when my life calms down, I want a big old dog that loves people. I don't want him to protect me. I can do that myself." She shared a confident smile with the girls. "But a big old dog that just wants to be loved. Maybe a little goofy, too."

"Like Dreamer."

Sarah had to think about which child this was. "Who's Dreamer, Chloe?"

"I'm Kristi," the girl corrected her. "But that's okay, everybody mixes us up sometimes. It's all right. Dreamer is our friend's dog."

Was it all right? To have people constantly confusing your identity? Sarah had no idea.

Chloe went on. "Except mostly it's so much fun to fool people and we can do it so good! I'm mostly like Kristi, until we talk, and then Kristi is more like Nomi, but if I'm really careful and slow down and don't get so bossy, then I can almost be like their voices, too."

"You like fooling people?" Sarah asked, lifting her brow.

"Love it!" declared Chloe, arching her brow just like Sarah did. Same one, too. The left one. "Mama Gina says it's okay once in a while, but—" she hopped up and planted her hands on her hips, then tilted her head "—don't do it too often, missy, or folks won't trust you. And it's good to have folks trust you."

"She does a solid imitation of my mother." Renzo smiled at the little girl as she flopped back onto the carpet, and tucked herself back into the curve of his left arm.

"Well, mostly 'cause I love Mama Gina so much!" Chloe exclaimed. "She makes us so many good things, like cake and pie and sometimes grilled cheese with no burned spots!" She quickly turned her head back toward Sarah. "Can you make those things, too?"

"I can manage the grilled cheese, but I do sometimes have to scrape off the burned edges," Sarah admitted. The admission pained her, as if she was falling short because she couldn't make a perfect grilled cheese sandwich.

"Renzo makes really good grilled cheese," Naomi assured her. "He can teach you! Okay?"

"Happy to oblige, Doctor."

She'd been looking at the girls. She lifted her gaze when he spoke. Locked eyes with him. And when she did, she didn't want to unlock eyes with him. The compassion in his gaze drew her, but she'd seen the firm side of him earlier. He wasn't going to let this go without a fight. She was ready, but it had to be a genteel fight. Looking at Renzo Calloway, there wasn't a whole lot one would call genteel about the big cop. As if to confirm that impression, the bawling of the cows increased in volume before ebbing slightly again.

"Are they always this noisy?" she asked, frowning. "The cows, I mean."

"Because we're almost never, ever too noisy," Naomi told her sincerely. "Most of us, anyway." She darted a quick look toward Chloe, but Kristi interrupted before Chloe could take the bait.

"I love your fancy polish so much." Kristi put her chin into her hands and gazed longingly at Sarah's nails. "They're so bee-you-tiful."

"I can only do fancy when I'm not working," Sarah told her, "so I thought I'd get them pretty before I came here on vacation." There was a world globe sitting on the nearby end table. She pointed to a dot alongside the word *Seattle*. "This is where I live." She had to take a deep breath before she said this next part. "Your mom was adopted by a family in Wenatchee, and I was adopted by a family in Seattle."

"Because nobody wants two kids," declared Chloe in a knowing voice. Her statement made Sarah flinch because her parents would have taken both girls in a heartbeat if they'd been told. But they weren't, and that meant Sarah had gone one way and Jenn another. If it wasn't for the rise of DNA testing, she might have never known that she had a sister.

"I think there are lots of people who would love more than one child," Sarah began, but Chloe cut her off.

"I heard Miss Samson tell Mama Gina that she was *real glad* our mama took care of things because most folks only want one kid." She raised her shoulders in a very expressive shrug. "Mama Gina said God sent three of us, so why would people only want one? That's so silly!"

"It's very silly, dear. You're smart to realize that," Sarah replied.

"Which is why all three girls are here with us," the

good-looking cop reminded her. "We had the room and the family and the love for all three. Jenn was my friend and neighbor. I grew up with her." His eyes darkened slightly. "When she lost her mother, they went through a real hard time, but we went through it together, like we always did. Because she mattered to us. Her mother was my mother's best friend." He didn't get emotional as he spoke, but he didn't have to. She saw it in his face. His expressive blue eyes, the kind of eyes that could melt a woman's heart. She'd have to be careful around this man. His strength. His charisma. And those beautiful eyes.

"When the girls' grandfather wasn't able to take custody of them, we considered it an honor to step in and that's how it's been," he told her. "Although the diaper thing was out of control for a while, but we're beyond that now, and I can't say I miss it." He winked at the girls and they giggled. "My mother and Jubilee Samson would never have let the girls be split up. Maybe things are different now, Sarah."

"As they should be," she said softly. She wouldn't argue. She rarely argued. It was much better to bring facts to the table that made argument useless. "So, girls, your mother was raised here and I was raised not far from the Puget Sound, a beautiful body of water that separates Seattle from the ocean."

"We have lakes," Naomi told her.

"And Renzo takes us to the rivers," added Chloe.

"And I got all bit up by skeeters at the creek and Renzo forgot to put my bug spray on and he was real sorry," Kristi explained. "But I told him it only itched for a while."

"Mosquitoes rarely bother Naomi and Chloe, but they love Kristi. They like to think of her as a delicious lunch," he teased. "Who would expect that from three girls who share the same DNA?"

Sarah was already marveling at the differences between the girls, despite their identical genetics.

"So you live really far away from us?" asked Chloe, and it wasn't easy to see where her mind was trending, but Sarah was pretty sure there was a reason for the question.

"Not so far," she replied. "It's about three hours from here to my parents' home on Mercer Island, and a little less than that to my apartment in the city. I like to live close to where I work so I can get there in a hurry if they need me," she explained.

"Because you're important?" Naomi's winsome look made Sarah want to be special in these girls' eyes. She wondered for a moment what that said about her before she answered the question.

"We're all important, darling." Naomi's sincerity had grabbed her heart when she'd walked in the door. "I'm a doctor and I work on sick babies. Teensy, tinsy babies, like you guys were when you were born, I bet."

"She was the smallest." Naomi pointed to Kristi as if to set the record straight. "Then Chloe, and I was the biggest baby but still small I think. But not *as* small. But Chloe's oldest and no matter what, I will never, ever get to be older than her. Just bigger."

Chloe's smug expression indicated she liked being one up on her sisters.

Naomi reached over and touched Sarah's honey-toned hair. "We match."

The innocence of those two words made a difference because Sarah understood not matching only too well. Despite the gift of two loving parents, there had always been that question of *where did I come from? And why did they let me go?* "We do, don't we?"

"Bella matches us, too," Chloe declared. She got up and danced around the room as if sitting too long annoyed her. "And Stefan. And Jamie. So you're not the only one. But there are kids in school who don't match us, even a little. Like Gracie J. And she's my bestie."

"Those are kids in her preschool class," Renzo explained before he shifted his attention back to the girls. Suddenly his phone pinged an incoming text.

Chloe leaped to the sofa, snagged the phone and handed it to Renzo. "Is it about Papa? Is he okay? Is he coming home?"

He hesitated, scanned the message, then shook his head. "They've given him some medication to help him, and when he's feeling better, they're going to take him to a hospital that's near Aunt Sarah's home. Because he can get the best care there."

"And then he'll come home," said Naomi. "So we'll be extra good for Mama Gina while he's gone."

If he came home. And right now that was a big "if." Sarah studied the girls, then Renzo.

He didn't return the look. He grabbed a book off the

couch and read it to the girls, then read one more before he announced it was time for bed.

The message from his mother left him unsettled.

Your presence might have something to do with that, a few hours after you informed him that you want to take custody of the girls.

The truth resonated, and when he finished tucking the girls into bed, she faced him squarely. "I know this whole situation is awkward."

"You think?" He didn't mess around, and she liked that about him.

"Will your mother stay with your dad?"

"Yes, of course."

"And your brother will take care of the ranch and the angry cows?" She'd pushed the incessant bawling to the back of her mind, but now that the girls were in bed, the noise seemed to intensify.

"They'll quiet down in a day or two," he told her gruffly. Then he drew a breath. When he did that, he seemed full of life, nothing like the men she'd known in the city. "Listen, Sarah, my job makes me careful with words. If I say too much, a suspect goes free. If I say too little, I'm denying rights. So I'm cautious by necessity, but right now I'm weighing everything I say, wondering how you're going to use it against me in a court of law. I don't want to think about that with my father fighting for his life, my mother gone and the girls facing a possible tragic loss. I need a truce."

She locked eyes with him, and once again, she didn't want to break the connection. That was dangerous ground. "Terms?"

"I have vacation time coming, so I can take a short leave from the force, but I don't want to have to double-think everything I say. If you'd consider being on hand to help with the girls, get to know them, have time with them, I'd like to put the legal discussion on hold. Not because you don't deserve to be part of their lives. But because it's a lot to handle at this moment. And I think Mom's got enough on her plate, don't you?"

He was right.

She knew it. Understood it. But something ate away inside her at the thought. And yet—

He was sincere. She felt it. Believed it. So could she put her quest for custody on hold to help them through this situation?

Do you have a choice?

The question hit home.

She wasn't giving up on her goal of bringing her family back together. She was simply putting it on hold.

She drew a deep breath and reached out her hand. "Agreed. I didn't come here to cause division."

"You did," he corrected her softly, but he still took her hand. "But I'm pretty sure I'd be doing the same thing in your shoes. So for the moment, let's take time for the girls to get to know you and for our lives to settle back down. Okay?"

She was being foolish.

The time to stake a claim would be now. What court would award custody of three preschoolers to an older couple with severe health issues?

But when he gripped her hand, there was a part of her that wished he'd go on gripping it forever.

Clearly she'd been working too hard.

She tugged her hand back and faced him square. "Okay. But on one condition."

He waited, and she had to hand it to him. He didn't have a "tell" and if he did, he was good at keeping it under wraps. "And that is?"

"My mother's in town," she told him. "She's a wonderful person, and she's going to want to be involved. Just so you know, there is absolutely no way of stopping her. And you have to be okay with that."

His gaze relaxed. A hint of a smile eased his jaw. "Yes, bring your mother along. Family is family, and my mother would skin me alive if I didn't put out the welcome mat. I'll put a call into work and then I'll see you tomorrow, okay? Bright and early. They sleep soundly, but they don't sleep late. We'll be flipping pancakes by 7:00 a.m."

He wasn't just allowing her access. He was swinging the door wide-open, and she hadn't prepared herself for that. Or for the way her heart had reacted when he'd read that text from his mother. When sorrow had filled his gaze. Sorrow he'd tamped down when he faced the girls with false calm. "We'll be here. And Renzo?"

"Hmm?"

"Thank you."

He winced. Then scrubbed a hand across the nape of his neck and sighed softly. "See you tomorrow."

Chapter Four

"You failed to mention that he's gorgeous," Lindsay Brown whispered when she caught sight of Renzo the next morning. He must have seen their car pull in because he'd called for them to come in when they reached the front door. The scent of pancakes and warm syrup offered an explanation why when they stepped inside and crossed to the kitchen. Lindsay sent Sarah a look of surprise, but when Renzo turned around, her mother's face was serene, a trick Lindsay Brown did well.

"I hear footsteps," he warned as he flipped a pancake without using a spatula. He simply gave an upward jerk to the griddle and the pancake went up, turned over and came back down.

"Unbelievable." Her mother knew her way around a kitchen, unlike Sarah, so when her eyes rounded, it was utterly sincere. "That's impressive, right there."

"Renzo Calloway," he told her with a smile that widened when footsteps came their way. "Nice to meet you, ma'am." The calves and cows could still be heard bawling outside, but they'd moved farther from the house so the noise wasn't quite as deafening today. "Here come the girls."

The triplets clattered down the broad, open stairs and when her mother spotted them, she sat right down on a kitchen chair and cried.

"Mom?" Sarah squatted next to her, alarmed. She thrust a paper napkin from the table into her mother's hand and all three girls paused, uncertain what to do. "Mom, are you okay?"

"I can't believe it," she whispered, then swiped the tears from her eyes and replaced them with a bright smile. "Girls, you look so much like Sarah did when she was little. It just took me by surprise."

"We look like *our* mom," Chloe corrected her. Then she raced across the room, snatched Jenn's picture from the table and brought it back. "See?"

"Chloe June." Renzo's tone was calm, but it held warning.

The name put a flush in the girl's cheeks, which was all it took to wipe the sassy tone from her voice.

"Oh, she's so beautiful, isn't she?" Lindsay admired the picture with a warm look. "She and Sarah look a lot alike. That's not always the case with sisters," she told them.

"It's not?" Naomi looked skeptical. So did Kristi. Chloe still looked a little combative.

Lindsay pulled out her phone and drew up a photograph. "These are my sisters. That's Carolina and that's Leslie."

"They don't look like you even a little bit," Chloe

observed grudgingly. "Are you sure they're your sisters?" she pressed.

"Except this one has pretty eyes like you," noted Naomi, pointing toward Leslie.

"Naomi notices everything," said Renzo as he flipped another pancake onto a platter. "It's her nature. A born reporter."

His words made Naomi preen.

"Carolina looks like our mom," Lindsay explained. "Leslie looks like our Dad. And I look a little like both, but mostly like my grandma. Isn't that funny?"

"Weird." Chloe made the pronouncement in a quiet voice, but Renzo heard it.

"Not weird. Genetics," he told her. "Pancakes are ready, ladies."

"With apples from CeeCee's farm?" asked Naomi.

"Yes, ma'am."

"Apple pancakes are my bestest favorite of all," breathed Kristi. "Thank you, Renzo!"

"You're welcome, kid."

"Did Mama Gina call?" Naomi moved closer to Renzo's side. "How is Papa?"

Her question made the other girls pause to hear the answer. All three seemed a little guilty that they hadn't asked first thing.

"Mom said he's resting."

Those were his words. His eyes told a different story.

"We'll know more in a few days," he promised them. "It takes time for the brain to heal. Sometimes a long time."

"When Papa comes home, everything will be all

right again." Sarah wasn't sure which child spoke, but when all three exchanged looks, she realized they were bright children, and none of them assumed that everything was really going to be all right ever again.

"In the meantime, Aunt Sarah and I have everything under control," Renzo told them as he handed out two pitchers of maple syrup. One was real. One was flavored. And to Sarah's surprise, the girls had very different ideas on how they liked their apple pancakes.

Naomi picked up the real maple syrup.

Chloe picked up the bottle of maple-flavored syrup and applied more than any child should have in one day.

And Kristi simply buttered her pancakes with real butter, then shook powdered sugar over them with an old-fashioned sifter.

Once the girls dug in, all three agreed these were the best apple pancakes they'd ever had. When Renzo finished cooking the last two, he made a dubious face at them. "You say that every time so you can sweet-talk me into making them again."

"Well, Mama G. kind of burns them."

"Because she's so busy," Naomi explained, as if his mother needed defending.

"And then she cuts off the burned part," added Kristi around a mouthful of pancake.

"But you can still taste it and that's not the best."

"And Papa can't cook at all." Chloe kind of snorted the words, as if teasing Renzo's father. Then she remembered what happened. Tears suddenly filled her eyes. She didn't cry, though. She blinked them back, and Sarah glimpsed herself in the child's stoicism.

"Mrs. Brown, would you like pancakes?" Renzo asked.

"Call me Lindsay, please, and I'd love some."

"What about you, Sarah?"

He turned her way. *Strength and compassion.*

That's what she read in his gaze. The kind of man who was strong enough to be gentle. A leader.

His phone pinged just then. Then it rang, almost simultaneously, and the ringtone was a catchy dance tune.

"Uh-oh." Kristi made a silly face. "I think that's your girlfriend, Renzo!"

All three girls giggled, and Sarah put a firm clamp on her quick reaction to Renzo's big blue eyes.

He tossed a fake frown at the girls. "She's *not* my girlfriend. We just work together." Then he answered the phone, walking into the other room with it, so Sarah couldn't hear what he was saying.

When he came back, his brow was drawn tight. Too tight. As if the big guy had the weight of the world on his shoulders.

The back door pushed open just then. A chill wind blew through the cozy kitchen, and Renzo's brother stepped into the room. He spotted her, then her mother, but didn't bother with pleasantries. He looked straight at Renzo. "I texted you from the barn. Will these gals mind watching the girls while you help me with chores?"

Renzo was angled away, so the girls and his brother missed his look of frustration.

Not Sarah. And when he turned to face his brother, he'd wiped it clean. "Sarah, are you okay here for about two hours?"

"We're happy for the chance to get to know the girls." Sarah smiled at them.

"And I can echo the girls' compliments, Lorenzo." Lindsay smiled up at him from her seat. "These are the best pancakes I've ever had."

The compliment didn't seem to make him uncomfortable. He flashed her a quick, sincere smile. "Not burning them does help. My competition is somewhat weak in that department, but she makes great stew." He turned toward his brother. "I'll be right there."

Kyle gave his brother a long, slow look, then stepped back. "I'll go get started."

He walked out, still not acknowledging her mother or chatting with the girls. Was he a jerk or just totally stressed?

Sarah didn't know, but you didn't get through med school and residency without an occasional face-off. In the end, those confrontations might have prepared her for her biggest fight of all: seeking custody of her sister's children.

Renzo tugged on a couple of layers of clothes and thick, waterproof boots. Resolve sculpted the planes of his face.

"Will the cows stop crying soon?" Kristi asked. "I'm so sorry for them right now because they just want to be with their mamas."

"I don't know why everyone can't be with their mama," Chloe grumbled under her breath. She darted a dark look in the direction of the lowing cattle, then Sarah. "I don't believe that God should ever take mamas away."

"I know," Naomi agreed, suddenly glum, and for just a moment, Sarah wondered what to say, what to do.

But then Renzo got down on one knee between Chloe and Naomi. "I don't have answers for why people get sick," he told them firmly. "But I do know that God puts people in our path to make things better. To love us. To cherish us. And when your grandpa was too sick to take care of you guys, he knew you had a home with us for as long as you needed because that's what you do when you love someone. You help them. You care for them. It's not the same, I know." His phone pinged a text right then, but he didn't pull it out. Instead, he took the time to stretch an arm around the girls and kiss each forehead in turn, then reached around Naomi to do the same with Kristi. "But it's still a blessing."

"I love you, Renzo!" Naomi threw her arms around his neck. "So much! You are the best person in the whole wide world!"

"Triple best." Kristi scrambled down from her chair and made it a group hug. Chloe followed. She didn't speak, but she hugged him fiercely, and when he stood, all three girls clung to him like monkeys in a tree, laughing and gripping in what seemed to be a familiar game as he pretended to try to shake them loose.

"Gotta go." He made eye contact with Naomi.

She nodded and slid off without prodding. Kristi did, too. Only Chloe clung tight, and when she locked eyes with Renzo, Sarah's chest squeezed because the look they exchanged was raw pathos. He hugged Chloe close, whispered something in her ear, then eased her down.

She looked up at him. Then Sarah. Then nodded.

He smiled, palmed her head and turned. "I'll be back shortly. I'll text if I need to. Feel free to do the same."

Sarah stood up and took a step toward him. Just one, and while moving toward this man felt right, he was going to be a major obstacle in her goal, so she paused after that initial step. "And we'll be here, waiting."

He gave her a crisp nod, then offered a tiny salute to her mother. "It is a pleasure, ma'am. And I mean that sincerely."

"Mine, too," replied her mother, and when he'd gone through the side door, Lindsay turned to her daughter. She whooshed out a breath, then stood and crossed to the coffee maker. "Not that I'm pushing, but this guy scores a solid ten in a couple of departments. And bonus points in others." She whistled softly under her breath so only Sarah would hear.

"Mom…"

"If he makes a solid pot of coffee," Lindsay announced, "I will be absolutely over the moon. Coffee, apple pancakes and three wonderful girls?" She flashed Sarah a smile. "I'm all in."

So was Sarah, but she'd seen the expression that Renzo hid from the girls. From his brother.

He hid pain.

Well, so did she, but she'd had no choice in the matter that brought her here yesterday. One way or another, she was going to fix a mistake that had happened over thirty years before, and nothing—and no one—would stop her.

Kyle didn't need his help, Renzo thought as he descended the back steps. He *wanted* Renzo's help, and that was what separated the two brothers lately.

He moved toward the barn through the thin morning

fog. Huge, nearly marketable calves bawled to his left. On his right, the mamas called out their lament. Folks often thought winter calving was the toughest part of beef production in a northern climate, and while guiding cows to safe areas in bad weather wasn't a picnic, he'd grown up doing it and he did it well.

For him the seventy-two hours of incessant lowing cattle was the challenge, but in two days the big calves would go one way, the cows would go another, and all would be well. And he respected the way his father kept the calves with their mothers for an extended period of time. His father liked the natural order of things, and never rushed anything.

Kyle was different.

He seemed to seek change for the sake of change. He wanted everything easier. Shorter. Faster. But some things couldn't be rushed, and raising cattle was one of those things.

Kyle had loaded up the forks on the old John Deere. He was moving toward the cows' side of the grazing area with a round bale of hay. That left Renzo to supplement the restless nine-month-olds on the lower side of the fencing. He'd attend to the creep feed, the soy supplement that raised the protein levels of their daily rations. In ranch-speak, he got the tougher job because he was Kyle's underling on the ranch and his brother enjoyed that.

He got the job done without losing a calf through the double-gated system on the way in. Leaving the grazing area was easier. The calves' interest in the fresh meal took precedence, and he brought the smaller tractor around to the graveled barnyard.

Kyle was already in the barn. A watering system had started leaking the week before, and they hadn't gotten around to fixing it. Kyle thrust his chin toward the rusted coupler. "I figured we'd get that done next."

Renzo pointed to the well-lit house two hundred feet away. "Have at it. I've got three kids that need watching."

"But their aunt is there."

Renzo did a slow count to five in his head, because there was no way he'd make it to ten. "A woman they met last night while Dad was on the floor, fighting for his life. And I'm supposed to stay out here and help you while they worry about Dad?" He was four inches taller than Kyle, and he locked eyes with his shorter brother. "Not gonna happen. The girls need me. You don't."

"Didn't expect you'd be much help out here, anyway. If you'd wanted to be, you'd have stayed here and built the ranch up like we promised Dad a long time ago."

Leave it to Kyle to go for the jugular with a conversation they'd had many times. "We were kids, Kyle. Ranch kids. And then we grew up. It's all right that I took a different road. Mom and Dad understood it. I wish you did."

Kyle muttered something under his breath, but strode away as if Renzo wasn't worth the time, but that had been his brother's attitude for a while. Was he unhappy on the ranch? Or unhappy everywhere? Their father had been their buffer, and because he was so good on the ranch, Kyle never had to stretch. Now he had to, and he wasn't happy with that.

The sun began breaking over the arch of the trees. Its warmth stirred the fog, then it lifted, swept into the atmosphere by the rising temperature. The ranch splayed out before him. His grandfather had started Calloway Ranch nearly seventy years ago. It had been a side job for a man who worked construction in the rapidly growing urban area of Quincy, Washington. His father and grandfather had built the ranch into a self-supporting business. A rural lifestyle that fit their proximity to Golden Grove and the nearby city.

Renzo loved the life, but he'd never tipped his hat toward ranching. He was a lawman, through and through. His blood ran lawman blue, and he was all right with that. So was his father.

Not Kyle, but that was his problem. Only now it was Renzo's problem, too. One man could handle this operation. Sixty cows on a regular cycle weren't that time-consuming, especially at this time of year. Would Kyle rise to the task? Could he?

Renzo wasn't sure, and if he wanted his father to have a business to come home to, he'd have to help, but it would be on his terms.

It won't, his conscience scolded lightly, *because you know Kyle's focus is split somehow and that will only cause your father more worry. When he's healthy enough to worry, that is.*

Whatever was going on with Kyle wouldn't be solved quickly, but Renzo's first concern had to be the girls. He shed his coveralls in the back entry, started a load of laundry to keep the barn smell out of the house and headed inside.

The scent of deliciousness swamped him.

Lindsay was working at the stove in the now-clean kitchen. Sarah had the girls around the big table. Heads down, they were busy with the project at hand. Glue sticks, washable markers, glitter pens and construction paper covered the old oak boards.

Intent on their work, the girls didn't notice him come in.

Sarah did. She looked up. Their eyes met, and when they did, his angst about Kyle was quickly forgotten.

Winsome eyes. Beautiful. Filled with compassion and strength. He was drawn to both, a draw he'd firmly resist because things were already convoluted enough.

Kyle was too self-interested to understand the change that Sarah brought into their lives. Or maybe, being slightly removed, it didn't worry him the way it bothered Renzo. Kyle loved the girls in his own way, but he'd never taken much part in raising them. He and Valerie seemed quite content to be the fond aunt and uncle, cheering from a distance.

Renzo had been hands-on from the beginning. From the time Naomi came home from the hospital. Then Chloe. And finally, Kristi, with her long list of needs. He and his mother had worked out a schedule. He'd rearranged his work hours. He'd stood tall and strong when others were too busy, and they'd successfully nurtured three preemies into the healthy, happy girls at the table.

Sarah was about to change everything, and he was

powerless to stop it, but even if he could, would he? Should he?

"Uncle Renzo, look!" Naomi spotted him and raised a piece of decorated construction paper. "We're making cards for Papa! So he knows we love him so much!" Joy filled her face.

"See mine?" Chloe's was more sedate, the product of her more analytical mind.

"And mine is beautiful, too." Kristi had gone all in with glitter and sequins. She pointed to the freshly glued sparkly circles. "I wanted him to be able to feel the pretty, even if his eyes are closed."

Kristi had been receiving occupational therapy for the past year, and tactile reactions had been polishing her fine motor skills. She still struggled some, but she'd come a long way.

"I love it," he told her. "What a great idea." Then he looked at Sarah. "This is wonderful," he added. "Thank you for thinking of it. It will give Mom and Dad comfort."

His phone rang just then. "It's Mom," he said out loud, then moved to the big living room beyond them. "Hey, how are we doing?"

"They're flying Dad to Seattle right now," she told him. "I'm going by car."

"Not alone, you're not," he replied swiftly. "One of us needs to be with you."

"Renzo, you know your father," she replied. She maintained an amazing level of calm, but then she always did. "He'd be more upset that the cattle weren't cared for, or that the girls were left on their own. You stay there. Kyle can run the ranch, and you mind the girls. That way Dad doesn't worry and neither do I."

"But—"

"Aunt Shelly is driving," she continued.

Aunt Shelly was his mother's younger sister. She'd lost her husband a year ago, and she and his mother were close.

"She'll stay with me, and it's as good for her as it is for me."

It was a solid plan. He knew that, but it was hard to stand down from his role of protector. And yet he had a vital role right here, so he kept his comment light. "I don't know if Seattle can handle both Altobelli sisters."

"We'll find out." She paused and sighed. "Keep praying, Renzo. Don't stop. Okay?"

He heard the fear in her voice, but she was a firm believer in God's will, a concept Renzo questioned more often than he should. "I won't. But God and I will have some firm words if this doesn't go our way."

"And the sweet Lord will love you regardless," she answered softly. "Always has. Always will. Shelly is here. Gotta go."

"Drive carefully and keep me in the loop, okay?"

"Every step," she promised. "You and Kyle both. Kiss the girls for me, all right?"

"I will."

He disconnected the call and came back to the big dining table. "Mama Gina sends her love and kisses and says they're moving Papa to a bigger hospital. Probably to make room for all of these pretty pictures," he told them, because he didn't want to scare them with the real reasons.

"Then we'll make a lot," declared Chloe.

"We've got lots of paper," noted Sarah. She stood up and moved to the kitchen side of the big room. "And coffee," she said softly. "I expect you could use a cup. What's the update?" She kept her voice low so the girls couldn't hear.

"They're using an air ambulance to take him to Seattle. It's not good," he added softly. "But you know that."

She nodded. "I know. Do you think your mom should be alone?" she asked, and he shook his head.

"As always, Mom's putting Dad's needs first. She knows how worried he'd be about the girls and the ranch if Kyle and I were in Seattle with them. My aunt Shelly is there," he explained. "She's going to drive to Seattle with Mom. They're not just sisters. They're like best friends."

"A special bond, for sure."

The moment she said it, he realized how his words might sting. She'd never had the chance to be besties with her sister, or even see her. "It is. Sarah—"

"Coffee. Kids. Glitter." She pushed a mug into his hands. "That's where my focus is right now. And on whatever my mother managed to put into that oven," she added.

"Apple crisp," said Lindsay. "The back fridge was full of apples, so it made sense."

"Only to those who can find their way around a kitchen," said Sarah. "I must have stepped out of line when they were handing out that particular talent."

"Or because you were graced with so many other gifts," Lindsay told her. "One can only excel at so many things."

"I cook," said Renzo, then wondered why he felt the need to say it.

Lindsay shot him a questioning look.

He sipped his coffee and shrugged. "I've lived on my own for fifteen years and a man's got to eat. Of course, once the girls were born I spent a lot more time over here. It was an all-hands-on-deck situation."

"You guys have done your job well," Sarah replied.

Their job.

He knew exactly what she meant. The Calloways had been the temporary caretakers. Now she would step in. She said it nicely, but that didn't change her ultimate goal.

He looked at her. Then the girls. Then he squared his shoulders. "One thing you should know about me, ladies." He set the mug down. "When I tackle a job, I don't give up. And I never leave a job half-done."

He walked away and headed upstairs to wash up and grab some clean clothes.

His job was to watch over the girls and this home, to keep it all intact for his parents' return, and he had every intention of doing so, despite Sarah Brown.

Chapter Five

"You're drawing a hard line in the sand, Sarah." Her mother poured a fresh cup of coffee, and faced her daughter an hour later. The girls had piled into Renzo's SUV and gone to the grocery store with him.

Sarah was putting away the rest of the art supplies. She tucked things back where she'd found them, in labeled organizer drawers in a nearby closet, all low enough for the girls to reach easily. "There's no other choice, Mom."

"Oh, honey, there are always other choices. I'm not criticizing," she continued when Sarah frowned. "But imagine how hard it must have been for Jenn to be separated from you when you two were split up. She was only two years old when that happened. These girls are almost four. Their cognitive development is much further along and they love this family. I'm not asking you to change your objective." She crossed the narrow space and put her hands on Sarah's shoulders. "Just to think about it, step by step. The wrong move now could have traumatic results later on. That's not just my maternal side talking. The pediatric doctor in me urges the same caution."

Her mother had chosen a career in pediatric medicine long before they'd adopted Sarah. Her love for children seemed innate. How difficult it must have been to be unable to have her own children. "You've always taught me that kids are more resilient than grown-ups give them credit for."

"And I believe that's true," Lindsay replied. "But life's traumas can hit hard and linger for a long time. Being suddenly taken from the home they love and the people who raised them could be really tough on the girls. You don't want resentment and anger to ruin your relationship with them so early on."

Right now Sarah just wanted what had been denied her for over three decades. Her family. Her sister. A piece of her history that had been swept out from under her. "Nobody worried about that for me," she told Lindsay, and she gripped her mug extra-tight because it made her hands stop shaking. "Nobody thought of that when they sent my sister to Wenatchee and me to Seattle."

"And I can't even begin to tell you how angry that makes me," whispered Lindsay. She drew Sarah into a hug. "Your dad and I would have taken Jenn, too. We would have loved that, so being denied the opportunity to keep you two together infuriates me."

"I keep asking myself why," said Sarah. "Why would they think separating us was okay, even if there was a high demand for babies. And then I wonder if she ever cried for me. If she ever fell asleep wondering where her baby sister was. Because she was old enough to remember me, to miss me."

"Oh, honey." Her mother held her in her arms for long moments until Sarah pulled free. "Maybe it's a blessing that we don't remember much of those early years. But what I do know as a pediatrician is that sudden loss or change does have an effect on kids' psyches and even sometimes on their physical health. I don't want you to give up your goal," she pressed. "But I'm advising you to take time. Go slow."

"And my attorney just texted me that this is the best time to go ahead and file a custody suit because Mr. Calloway's poor health provides a window of opportunity. She cited Washington's law that gives relatives of children first priority in adoption and custody cases."

"Legally you're no relation to them," her mother reminded her.

"My DNA says otherwise," argued Sarah. "And I've gathered theirs to be tested," she admitted. "When they were brushing their teeth this morning."

"As if you need proof," Lindsay replied, but then she sighed. "This isn't right, Sarah. It's not wrong, but it's not right, either. You need a peaceful agreement with the Calloways. Maybe share custody."

"And split time with them? I've considered that," Sarah stated. "I don't want to mess these children up in any way, but the thought of shared custody has drawbacks, too."

"Sometimes it's the best choice," her mother told her. "Families compromise all the time."

Was such a thing possible?

It made sense. Even through her haze of anger, she had to put the girls' needs first, but could she share their future after being denied so much of her past? "I don't know if I'm that rational about the subject," she admitted.

"Then you need to get more rational," Lindsay advised. "Pray about it. Think it through. This is as important as any life-or-death surgery you've ever performed, Sarah. Because severing family ties isn't something that can easily be resutured. And that's all I'm saying."

"I hear you, Mom." Sarah set down her mug as she heard Renzo's SUV turn into the long driveway. "I'm just not sure I'm strong enough to do it."

"Then pray for strength." Lindsay took her hands. "The strength that's gotten you this far in your career is enough to guide you over this hurdle. Why hurt others when we don't have to, darling?"

Her mother was right, but over Lindsay's shoulder was that framed photo of Jenn, gone before she'd had a chance to know her. See her. Even just to hear her voice.

As the girls scrambled into the house, the look of them, so much like her and her lost sister, tipped the scales again.

She'd been foiled once, as an infant.

No one was going to foil her again.

Renzo never had to pretend to be grateful before. He'd had some serious ups and downs, and he'd faced some brutal situations on the job. Eighteen years of being a professional lawman ensured that, but he'd al-

ways been able to separate the grace of family from
the bad side of society. He'd helped countless people
over the years, before and after he became a detective,
and those good outcomes offset the rougher moments
of his profession.

But right now his father was fighting for his life, his
mother was gone, Kyle was acting like a self-absorbed
moron and the girls were about to be swept away by a
stranger and there was nothing he could do about any
of it. The whole thing was making him crazy.

So why was he leading three preschoolers through
a busy holiday-themed grocery store with all this rolling through his brain? Taking a tribe of small children
anywhere was a lot like herding cats. He realized that
as Tug Moyer called him. He pulled out the phone and
answered quickly while the girls were captivated by
a holiday-themed baking display. Tug wasn't only his
best friend, he was the newly elected county sheriff and
Renzo's former partner. "Hey, what's up?"

"I wanted news on your dad," Tug replied. "My
mother is bringing supper over tonight, and Christa
and the kids are baking you brownies with chocolate
chips because they said those are the best. And probably cookies, too." Tug's voice deepened. "How are you,
Renzo? How are you holding up? And how can I help?"

A *thunk* hit dead center in Renzo's chest, because
there wasn't anything anyone could do. "I don't think
you can," he admitted. "No one can. Dad's prognosis
is terrible, Kyle's being a jerk and the girls' long-lost
aunt has shown up out of the blue and wants custody of
them, which a smart judge will probably grant because

there is no reason on earth not to. And that's just been the past forty-eight hours. So how's *your* day going?" he quipped, knowing Tug's day had to be better, because it couldn't be worse.

"An aunt?" Tug repeated. "There is no aunt, Renzo. Jenn was an only child. Adopted."

"Well, it seems there were two children adopted that day, one to a family in Seattle, and Jenn to the Drews. Jenn died without knowing she had a sister, and the sister discovered the relationship through a DNA service. Now she's here to restore her family, and I can't even hate her for wanting to do that. Believe me, I've tried to dislike her. It's quite impossible. Did I mention she saved Dad's life when he crashed on the living room floor?" he added.

"Renzo." Tug paused a moment. "Man, I'm so sorry. I don't have easy words. I can't soften any of this stuff with your dad, and I can't imagine what's going on with Kyle, but I can run interference with this woman. Do a background check on her. Make sure she's legit. Let me take over on that, and—"

"No." Tug meant well, and Renzo knew he'd go to the ends of the earth for him, but he couldn't have him investigate Sarah. "She's so beyond legit as to make us look like criminals. She totally looks like Jenn. Even has those same quiet gestures. I thought I was seeing a ghost when I found her taking pictures of the girls at the park. No, don't investigate her. She's actually staying here for a few weeks to help. Her and her mother. They'll get to know the girls, and the girls will get to know them." The triplets seemed to reach a mutual agreement about something at that moment. They turned en masse and headed his way. "Gotta go. I'm shopping with three little kids, and my time is up. Come by the ranch, though, Tug, okay? I want you to meet her. I want your opinion to make sure I'm not being snowed."

"No one has ever snowed you, Calloway. Well, except Kitty Carson in eleventh grade—"

"Hey! I was sure I'd found true love, but she only wanted me to get even with her college boyfriend." The memory made him almost smile. It had seemed so tragic then. "Lesson learned."

"I'll come by this week. Where's your mom staying in Seattle? We want to send flowers," Tug continued. "To her and your aunt. Brighten their room."

Renzo gave him the hotel name as the girls gathered around him. He put away the phone and looked down.

Chloe held up holiday-themed cupcake liners. "Can we get these, Renzo? They're so cool!"

"With snowflakes on them!" added Kristi.

"And can we get marshmallow snowmen, too?" said Naomi. "So they can march around the kitchen keeping everyone safe." She pretended to march down the grocery aisle, drawing smiles from other shoppers.

"Do they make marshmallow snowmen?" he asked, but when the girls led him back to the baking kiosk, he saw that they did.

"We want to bake stuff to send to Mama G.," Chloe explained. "If it's cheerful, she won't worry about us."

"Not one little bit!" insisted Naomi. "She'll know we're having fun."

"And we can still pray for Papa all the time," Kristi assured him. "Even while we're making stuff."

Bless their hearts. Leave it to their sweet natures to combine holiday fun with altruism. He nodded and motioned to the cart. "Let's get a bunch of stuff and that way Uncle Kyle or I can take them a delivery every few days, okay?"

"Can we come, Renzo?" Chloe gripped his arm in her classic ironclad grasp. "We'll be so good. We promise!"

"No kids allowed on his unit, sweetness, so no. You have to wait until he's better," he told her. "But if we take good care of Aunt Shelly and Mama G., then they can take good care of Papa. All right?"

"And you'll tell her how much we love her?" Chloe persisted. "And that we'll never, ever go away?" She met his gaze, and he met her eye to eye and lied to her for the first time ever.

"I'll tell her."

"Promise?" she demanded.

Leave it to Chloe to realize there was more at stake than a friendly family visit going on. "I promise. Let's get this done and get back home so you guys can start projects."

He let the girls pick an assortment of decorations for gingerbread houses, including the marshmallow snowmen, decorated cupcake liners and holiday sprinkles. And some harvest-themed candies for Thanksgiving. When they were done, the cart was full of baking essentials and several nonessentials, as well.

He paid for the groceries at the cashier while the

girls helped bag everything as best they could, then they carted it all home. When the girls lugged in bag after bag of baking supplies into the kitchen, Sarah stood there watching them, her arms wrapped around her waist. Then she smiled. First at them. Then him. And when she did, something soft and undeniably sweet hit him in the chest, especially when she lifted one eyebrow in his direction and posed a question to him. "Please say you like to bake. At least a little, okay?"

"I do, actually."

She brushed a hand to her forehead for the girls' benefit. "Phew!"

"You don't know how to bake anything? Like anything at all?" Kristi looked up at Sarah, dumbfounded.

"Not even brownies in a box?" asked Naomi.

"I bet our mother could bake everything," muttered Chloe, just loud enough to be heard. "I bet she liked doing things like that all the time."

"Well, I can learn," Sarah assured her. "I'm pretty smart, and how hard can it be?"

"That's what I tried to tell her," Naomi indicated Chloe as she set four packs of marshmallow snowmen on the counter. "But Chloe doesn't always like to listen to people."

"Well, Chloe and I have that in common," Sarah confessed. "I tend to go my own way, too, even when it might be way easier to learn from the mistakes of others."

Chloe didn't look at Sarah, but Renzo spotted the girl's thoughtful expression. She erased it quickly. "I think we can bake some stuff for Thanksgiving, and then Christmas cookies, okay? And send them to Mama G.? And Papa, if he can eat them."

Sarah bent low and surveyed all the baking essentials. "I think that's a marvelous idea. And while I'm not a great baker, my mom is, and I take really good pictures. How about if I take videos of you guys making things? And then we can send little movies to Mama G., too?"

"That is such an excellent idea!" Kristi grabbed her in a hug. "Then they can see us and maybe Mama G. can take pictures of them eating everything and send them back! Can we ask her, Renzo? Please?"

"Of course. And Sarah, she'd be over the moon if you did that." He'd crossed the room to tuck the milk and eggnog in the refrigerator. She'd done the same with three dozen eggs, and there they were, at the fridge, hands full, but neither one was looking at the fridge. She was looking up at him.

He was looking down at her.

His throat went tight. So did his chest, and when she quirked a smile his way, he had to smile back. It wasn't her beauty that drew him. It wasn't her relationship to three children he loved.

It was her.

She was clearly brilliant. No one got that far in medicine without being brilliant, but she didn't laud her intelligence or her degrees. She was down-to-earth, and that amazed him. Frankly, *she* amazed him, and he wondered what it would be like to close the gap between them.

He shut that thought down swiftly, but as they loaded

the refrigerator, the scent of her surrounded him. Floral and fruity. As she leaned forward to position the eggs, her hair fell forward, too.

Was it as soft as it looked?

He guessed that it was, but right now his options weren't just limited. They were nonexistent. With Dad's condition and Kyle's attitude, everything Roy Calloway and his father had built could come crashing down, and then what would his father have to come back to?

Nothing.

Renzo couldn't let that happen.

He backed away from Sarah, not because he wanted to. Instinct was pulling him in a very different direction. But because he had to, and that was a different situation altogether.

Chapter Six

Renzo Calloway captivated her like no one had ever done before, Sarah admitted to herself a few days later. That was the last thing she expected to happen while she was in Golden Grove. And something to be avoided at all costs. The guy was a trained detective. A cop. He was probably running a background check on her right now, and yet...

He seemed utterly sincere. Was he? Or was he just well-practiced on how to get people to let their guard down?

Well, it wouldn't work with her, she decided as she disconnected from a conference call she'd had to take. She'd come to Golden Grove with one objective: to fill the empty hole the adoption had created. There would be fallout for the Calloways. She didn't want to cause sorrow, but the blame didn't lay on her.

The girls were at preschool. Renzo was running errands, then would pick them up when their classes let out. Her mother had popped out to get a hair trim, leaving Sarah ninety minutes before anyone would return. So when the side door opened, she crossed the kitchen quickly to see who was coming in. In Seattle, people didn't just walk into houses. The opposite was true here.

A woman came in. A woman who seemed somewhat familiar. She looked at Sarah with that same look of surprise she'd seen on others' faces when they noted her resemblance to Jenn. "You're Sarah?"

"Yes," she answered. "Sarah Brown."

The woman moved forward. "I'm Valerie. Kyle's wife. I wanted to meet you while it was quiet. That doesn't happen often with three kids running around."

An awkward silence ensued. Valerie had way more right to be here than Sarah did, and yet the woman hesitated, as if waiting for an invite. Finally Sarah asked, "Do you want coffee? Or tea?"

"No. I was looking for Kyle but he's not in the barn, and I realized that the girls would be at preschool—"

"And you wanted to meet the person who showed up out of the blue to stake a claim," Sarah guessed.

To her surprise, Valerie shook her head. "Not at all. Well, I did want to meet you, but who wouldn't pursue something like this, in this day and age? What kind of person wouldn't want to follow through and find out about their history? And the girls?" she asked rhetorically. "I can't imagine it."

Sarah sat down. So did Valerie. Then Valerie slipped off her coat, placing it on the chair behind her. Friend? Or foe?

Sarah had no way of knowing, so she stayed neutral. "There are always choices. But when I realized that

Jenn and I had never even been told of the other's existence, I went looking for her online. And that's how I found out that my only sister had died and left three little girls. That made it a no-brainer," she stressed. "I'm determined to make this as right as I possibly can. I couldn't pretend that it was just bad circumstances because it wasn't. It was deliberate and misleading to everyone concerned. My parents would have gratefully taken both of us. But they were never given the chance."

"There will be heartache, Sarah," Valerie said frankly. "Kyle's parents didn't just love Jenn, they were her godparents. They were best friends with her mother and father, and they take the girls to see their grandfather regularly. Not as often now because his condition is deteriorating, but they've always wanted them to have a sense of family."

"I'm their family, too," Sarah replied. "Yes, it'll be hard on everyone. I know that," she went on, "but the girls deserve to have their biological family as part of their lives. Now that we know about one another. Do you have kids, Valerie?"

It was the wrong question.

She knew it the minute the words came out of her mouth, but there was no way to snatch them back.

Valerie's face went flat, and there was no denying the bleak look in her pretty brown eyes. "No." She seemed about to say more, then didn't.

A tear trickled down her left cheek. Then her right. She clapped a hand to her face as if to stifle them, but the tears kept coming. Sarah stood, crossed the room and brought back a box of tissues. She set the box in front of Valerie. "I'm sorry. I didn't mean to pry or be insensitive."

Valerie grabbed a clutch of tissues and mopped her face. Then she blew her nose and shook her head. She stood. "You weren't. I'm just on edge these days. It'll pass." Tears bubbled up once more. "It always does." She grabbed her jacket and hurried out the door. A few seconds later, a car engine started up and Valerie drove away, toward their ranch-style house just up the road. And as Valerie's car turned into the driveway, Sarah suddenly realized why she looked familiar. She'd seen her a few months ago at her friend Alvira's fertility clinic in Seattle. She'd been meeting Alvira for a quick supper and Valerie had been hurrying out, distraught.

Of course she hadn't asked Alvira about it. Not her patient, not her business, but she'd been dealing with anguished parents for nearly ten years, and she recognized the abject sorrow on Valerie's face then—and now.

And that was just one more thing she could do nothing about as she sought to fix the unfixable.

She hadn't thought she could feel worse about her decision to seek custody of the girls, but now—in light of all this family was going through—she did. And maybe that was the biggest surprise of all.

Renzo pulled into the driveway with the girls a little later. They ran into the house, waving construction paper turkeys and bird feathers, and by the time they'd organized their projects, had supper and gotten the girls washed and into bed, Sarah had newfound respect for all parents.

She came downstairs after one last round of good-night kisses and leaned against the counter. "If this were a commercial, the mom and dad would be cozied up by the fire, watching a movie and sharing a quiet moment. In reality—" she blew a lock of hair out of her face purposely "—any reasonable adult would totally crash at this point."

"Except a doctor on call doesn't always get that option, do they?"

Renzo posed a serious question. It deserved a serious answer. "No, which means I'll need to have a nanny on call when the girls are with me," she replied. "Or a live-in one, because you're right. My time isn't always my own."

"Or find a cute husband," Lindsay offered with a grin on her face. "Second choice gets my vote."

"I expect there are numerous prospects for either position," Renzo joked, but Sarah didn't miss the hint of seriousness behind his question. Was he wondering if she was dating someone?

"And I think we should talk. All of us." He motioned to her mother as he took a seat. "Some time when we're not exhausted. There's got to be a way we can share custody, Sarah. Because I think we should try to avoid breaking the girls' hearts."

"That's easy for you to say. You weren't the one affected by this whole thing," she replied.

He'd said they should talk when they weren't so tired. He was right, so she didn't take a seat now. The problems facing his family weighed heavily on her tonight, making it the worst possible time. She needed more than emotion to make decisions concerning the girls. She needed confirmation of her rights and legal standing as their biological aunt, despite their mother's wishes to have the Calloways raise the girls. And yet…

She moved to the door. "Mom. You ready to go?"

"Looking forward to a good night's sleep and back at it in the morning," Lindsay said cheerfully. She deliberately ignored the tension. She turned to Renzo and gave him a quick hug. "The girls are remarkable. You already know that."

He acknowledged that with a smile. "They're something, all right."

"You've done a great job. You and your family," Lindsay persisted. "I can't tell you enough how grateful I am for all you've done. You're amazing."

"It wasn't a job," he replied softly. "It's an absolute privilege." He shifted his attention to Sarah, behind her. "I've witnessed a lot of rough family stuff over the years. My work puts me in the thick of it, so I know it takes more than DNA to build a family. That doesn't mean I'm minimizing your rights, Sarah." He drew his brows together. "It just means that I'd like a peaceful resolution to this because it doesn't just mean a great deal to me, but to the folks I love."

She didn't respond. She turned and left, but as she climbed into her car, she had no choice but to face him as he stood in the doorway. He seemed oblivious to the nighttime cold, the chill wind. He stood, tall and strong, a perfect sentinel, standing guard, and as she reached to push the ignition button, she wondered… What would it be like to have her own personal hero standing by her side?

Weariness was affecting her judgment, a common malady. No doubt he'd return to normal human status when she saw him in the morning, but as she drove away, she couldn't erase that image from her mind.

Worse? She didn't want to.

Renzo pounded fence stakes into the ground a week later as he prepared to encircle the harvested cornfield for late fall grazing. It was a job that went quicker with two, but Kyle had disappeared and Sarah and her mom had taken the girls for new sneakers, although from the texts she'd sent him, it seemed more of an all-out shopping spree.

In picture after picture, the girls looked happy. Smiling for the camera, showing off their cute outfits, and somehow she'd gotten them to buy dissimilar clothes. He'd caved every time they pouted over not dressing alike and bought everything in triplicate.

Sarah was made of sterner stuff, it seemed.

And beautiful.

He tried to shove that thought aside as he rounded the last corner before stringing wire.

What was that all about? He'd known lots of beautiful women over the years. Lots of wonderful women.

Yet none called to him like her.

Was that because she was forbidden fruit? She was on the opposing team. She had a life in Seattle. A good life, he knew, because he'd done an internet search on her.

An eminent physician with a monster-sized education and the skill to operate on the tiniest babies. The very thought humbled him.

He was proud of his life. Proud of his career. He'd recently been promoted to detective, a job he loved. And now, more than ever, his parents needed all hands on deck.

A text came in just then. His mother sent a picture of his father in the state-of-the-art Seattle hospital. "Step by step!" read the caption, but the picture of Roy Calloway told more.

The stroke had aged him. He looked feeble, and the asymmetrical shape of his face indicated a slow recovery. *If* he recovered. He might be in top medical hands, but he'd suffered a major brain incident.

Renzo called his mother on video chat. If anything would help his dad recover, it would be to know things were plugging along at the ranch. "Hey, Mom and Dad. How's it going?" he asked in a bright voice, as if they were lounging on a beach somewhere.

His mother's excited voice came through loud and clear. "Honey, it's Renzo! Look!" She must have held the phone up for his father to see.

"Lookin' good, Dad!"

His father struggled to form words. None came. Renzo pretended that was all right and carried the conversation.

"I'm stringing fence right now." He panned the phone camera out so they could see his location. "The upper field is filled with the older cows, and we've moved the heifers to the front field." It was a maneuver his father did every year, to keep the first-time mothers closer to the barn. If one had a difficult birth, help was close at hand. "And it's cold!" He grinned into the camera. "We miss you guys, but we're getting on fine," he assured them. "The girls are missing you like crazy, and I've registered the calves for the post-Thanksgiving auction. And I've booked the cattle trucks for transport."

His father struggled to say something. Then to change expressions. Neither attempt worked and it broke Renzo's heart to see him struggle with such simple things.

"Tell them we love them." His mother's voice wavered slightly. "We love them very much and we'll see them soon. And tell them that Papa is getting better, a little bit at a time. And that he is very, very impatient," she added. Renzo was pretty sure she was making a face at his father right then.

"Skype us tonight," he told her. "Doesn't have to be long, but they'll be happier if they see you."

"I will," she promised. She changed the direction of her phone, but not before he saw the frustration on his father's face.

The sight unnerved him.

It shouldn't. He was a cop. He'd seen a lot worse. You didn't serve on the force for nearly twenty years without coming across grim scenes, but this was his father. His mentor. A beloved example of all things good.

He had to shove back a lump in his throat to keep his own voice from choking up. That would be the last thing either parent should hear. "Gotta go. You two keep up the progress there. We'll hold down the fort here. And we're having Thanksgiving dinner at the house."

"Did you invite Sarah?"

He had, somewhat reluctantly. Sharing childcare duties was one thing. Spending holidays together was a whole new level altogether, but he'd issued the invitation. "And her parents," he told her. "Her dad is driving inland on Wednesday. She says he stuffs a mean turkey."

"Renzo, that's very kind of you."

It didn't feel kind. Kindness would be if he *wanted* to share this holiday with these outsiders. He didn't, and yet he'd be 100 percent wrong not to have them spend the holiday in Golden Grove. He couldn't do that.

"Are Kyle and Valerie coming?"

"They're having dinner at her sister's place."

"Ah." That's all she said, but it was enough. She knew her sons well. Kyle and Valerie had missed a lot of family dinners over the past two years, ever since Kyle and Roy had disagreed about increasing the herd size. Kyle wanted to go bigger. Bigger meant a larger end-of-year paycheck, and for a ranch supporting two families, that would be wise.

But Roy resisted, insisting he couldn't handle the extra work. He didn't tell Kyle directly, but the message was clear. Roy was shouldering enough of the work as it was. No way did he want more.

Since then they'd worked together, but not with the closeness they'd once shared. The rift between them had widened as time went on. But it was their fight, Renzo had decided. He had enough on his plate with work and the girls. Only now he was thrust in the middle of it all, not by choice, but necessity.

He put away his phone, and by the time he'd strung the wire it was dark.

He'd seen Sarah, her mother and the girls return nearly two hours ago, and there was still no sign of Kyle. He'd left Renzo holding the reins again, much like he'd been doing with Dad. But Renzo would have to report back to work after Christmas, and there would be no backup for the ranch if Kyle didn't put his best foot forward.

What would happen then?

He headed toward the house, bone-tired. He shrugged out of his jacket and coveralls in the enclosed porch adjacent to the laundry room, set the washer going and stepped inside the kitchen.

"Surprise!" All three girls—in matching outfits—were waiting for him in the well-lit room.

Amazing smells hit him, a blend of fresh yeast and fragrant soup.

The girls piled on him, despite the fact that he had been working outdoors all day, and when he met Sarah's honey-toned eyes over their heads, he couldn't help but smile.

When she smiled back, his heart clenched again. Clearly it wasn't about to listen to his stern commands.

He stood. All three girls hung on, half-dangling from his arms. "Smells great in here."

"We made soup!" crowed Chloe.

"Like in the book we love, only without the stone because the stone wasn't the important part," Naomi explained. "It was all about sharing, Renzo! Everybody sharing something they had."

The girls loved the classic kids' story about a hungry

stranger who broached his idea of stone soup. It was a book his mother read to them often.

"Like potatoes or corn or other stuff," Kristi cut in. "They were so nice, and then everybody had food to eat and they loved it so much!"

"They said your mother read them that story," Sarah explained.

"How did you have time to make soup?" he asked. "It smells amazing, Sarah."

She blushed just enough to let him know that his words touched her. "Mom started it but she had to drive back to the coast for the night, so I finished it up myself. With firm advice via modern technology," she added, indicating her rose-gold phone sitting on the counter.

He inhaled fully and smiled. "Is that fresh bread I smell?"

"Now that *would be* extreme," she replied. "Frozen rolls from the grocery, but they smell marvelous, don't they?"

"Perfect," he told her, and he wasn't just talking about the soup and rolls any longer.

She studied him for a few seconds before dropping her gaze to the girls.

"We love you, Renzo!"

"Yeah, thank you for working so hard on the cows. When do those long trucks come?" asked Chloe. "Then the big babies can leave and we'll get ready for little ones."

"Right after Thanksgiving," he told her. "I've got it all set up."

"I will miss them so much." Kristi stared up at him.

"I don't want them to go far away and then people buy them and then people buy them and eat them. They're *our* cows, Renzo. Not anyone else's."

Oh, man.

He crouched down and faced her. "But if folks like eating meat," he offered reasonably, "someone's got to grow the meat. And isn't it nice that we take such good care of them, Kristi?"

"I think it's nice that we take good care of everything," she scolded him. "We take good care of Mittens and MoMo but we're not going to eat them."

Mittens and MoMo were their two barn cats. "Well, some farms grow potatoes. Or corn. Or wheat to make flour. We grow beef."

"It makes me sad," she whispered, giant tears filling her hazel eyes. "So sad, Renzo." She tucked her sweet face against his knit shirt and stayed there to hide her tears. He held her, wishing Sarah hadn't witnessed this. Would she use it in her plea for custody? That living on a beef ranch wasn't conducive to the girls' emotional well-being?

"Well, I'm not sad because I love it when the babies get born and Grandpa and Uncle Kyle fall in the mud and they carry babies up to the barn and they are so big and tall and strong like cowboys on TV," Chloe declared. "The big calves aren't fun anymore. I won't miss them at all."

"I might. A little," said Naomi. "But I'm glad they stopped bawling. Aren't you?" she asked Sarah.

She nodded, but there was no mistaking the sympathy in Sarah's gaze when she looked down at Kristi in his arms. "Yes. I've never heard that sound before. There aren't any beef ranches in the city. So hearing them cry was different. And sad," she added.

Great.

She'd probably been gathering all kinds of information she could use against his parents when the time came, and there was nothing he could do to stop it. Nor would he, he realized as he stood up, still holding Kristi. She and her mother had been good for the girls, and he wouldn't have been able to help Kyle without them.

When they eventually left, reckoning would come. He'd have to work. Kyle would have to muster up on the ranch and who was going to watch the girls? He could switch to afternoon shifts and hire a nanny. Kyle would be busy on the ranch, and Valerie worked in Wenatchee.

"You look tired." Sarah made the observation softly as Kristi wriggled to be put down. "The girls already ate. Can I offer you some soup? And rolls?"

"Give me ten?" He motioned down the hall. "I need to clean up."

"Of course. We'll do pajamas and teeth, right, ladies?" She smiled at the triplets and raised her arm. "Ready. Set. Go!"

They raced off. No argument. No fuss. No whining. "How did you do that?" He didn't mean for it to sound like a grumble, but it did.

She tapped the watch. "Competition. And they're not sure enough of me to give me a hard time over everything. Mom says when kids are confident in your love, they're self-assured enough to misbehave, so the girls are still on their best behavior with me."

"We've seen that before. And also the opposite, where kids we've fostered have been really bad to test the boundaries. See if my parents would give up."

"And did they?"

He nodded. "Twice. There was little choice, because the kids were doing dangerous things and needed a higher level of care. It crushed my mom to make that decision because her practical side is often at war with her emotional side. But in the end I think we all learned that we can only do our best."

"A hard lesson learned."

Compassion thickened her words. He thought about her job and winced. "I expect you've had your share of successes and failures, Sarah. Spending so much time in the NICU taught me a lot. We came home with three beautiful babies. Some folks experienced a very different outcome."

"I can't save them all," she told him as the clatter of kids' feet pattered over their heads. "But we save so many more than we used to, and I cling to that. And my faith," she added softly. "It helps."

"It sure does." He jutted his chin toward the spare room at the back of the house. "I'll be back soon." By the time he'd cleaned up and gotten changed, the girls were in matching pajamas, they'd each picked a book, and their faces and hands were scrubbed clean. "Mama Gina would approve," he told them.

His laptop buzzed and a picture of his mother flashed on the screen. "Hey. Look who's calling. Come here, girls." He answered the call and settled the laptop onto the living room table. "Hey, Mom. How's it going? How's Dad doing?"

Instantly the girls clamored to talk as they gathered around the small couch. "Mama Gina! We love you! We miss you this much!"

"Even more than that," declared Chloe, never to be outdone. "Like this much!" And she stretched her arms out as far as she possibly could.

"Can you come home and make cookies?" asked Naomi sweetly. "We'll help."

"No, Nomi, she's got to stay with Papa, you know that." Chloe went into instant boss mode. "We'll make cookies when Papa is better."

"Oh, my girls." Gina smiled into the camera. "I miss you so much. Papa is sleeping but he misses you, too. He needs lots and lots of rest right now."

"He can have my bed," offered Kristi. "I don't mind."

"Oh, sweetness, thank you. I'll tell him that," Gina promised. "Look at all of you. You look marvelous. And are those new pajamas?"

"With Christmas trees on them," crowed Naomi. "And pretty decorations."

"And ribbons!" added Kristi. "Aunt Sarah and her mom took us shopping and it was so much fun," she went on. "We bought everything. Well, like, almost everything," she corrected herself. "Renzo was busy with cows and stuff, but when our shoes didn't fit, Aunt Sarah said 'Hop in the car, girls. We must go shopping!'"

"Oh, tell her thank you." Sincerity laced his mother's

voice. "I knew your sneakers were getting tight, but I hadn't had a chance to buy them yet."

"You tell her, Mama Gina! She's right here! Aunt Sarah!" Kristi jumped off the couch, crossed to the kitchen and grabbed Sarah's hand. "Come see Mama Gina, okay? She wants to say thank you!"

"Yes, come over! Come over!" Naomi joined in the chorus. Only Chloe seemed to be aware of a quiet, underlying tension, but when Sarah moved forward, Chloe planted a peaceful look on her pretty face.

Sarah took a spot behind the couch.

Renzo moved over to the left, leaving Sarah and the girls to talk with his mother, and as Gina thanked Sarah for taking the girls shopping, he caught sight of the miniaturized image on the screen. Three blond girls and the blond woman.

They fit.

The girls looked enough like Sarah to be her own children, and for a moment it seemed like it was meant to be. And then Naomi got emotional. "I miss you." She swiped two tiny fists to her eyes as she stared at his mother's image on the computer screen. "I miss you so much, and Papa, too, but mostly I miss you and wish you could be here with us. It makes me so sad every day."

Her confession became instantly contagious.

Kristi's chin thrust out and her lips trembled. "Me, too," she whispered, as if it was hard to talk. "Every morning I think you'll be here but you never are and I just want you with us. All the time, Mama G."

Even Chloe had a hard time remaining stoic. "I miss you, too," she said softly, but then she caught hold of herself. "But I want Papa to get well, and you know Renzo is so good to us!" She threw her arms wide. "And he's good to the cows, too," she added. "And maybe he won't even have to go back to work again. Like ever."

He cleared his throat on purpose.

She darted a guilty look up at him.

"Well, the county will insist on me coming back to work after Christmas," he drawled, teasing. "But that's weeks away and we're doing fine, aren't we, girls?" He indicated Sarah with a hooked thumb. "Having Sarah and her mother here has been a huge help," he added, then said the words he didn't want to say. "I couldn't have done it without them."

He felt Sarah turn toward him, but he kept his eyes on his mother. Gina Calloway was a smart woman. She'd understand the depth behind his words, that Sarah was good for the kids.

"The Lord provides," Gina told them roundly. "In His way, He makes things known. He sends us what we don't even know we need. He blessed us with you, Sarah. Why else would you have shown up that day? At that hour? We owe you a great deal," she stated, then started blowing kisses into the camera. "I love you, girls. Sleep well and be good for Aunt Sarah and Renzo, all right?"

The girls promised to be good with lots of emotion in their voices, and when he reached out to disconnect the call, Chloe caught his hand. She didn't say a word, but watched the screen until Gina's image disappeared. And then she sighed.

He wasn't about to send them to bed on that note.

"One more story," he told them as he took a funny favorite off the nearby bookshelf. "And then bed, my sweet girls."

Sarah glanced at the cooling rolls and the pot of soup, but she didn't push. Soothing the girls took precedence over food right now.

She took a seat opposite the couch while he read the story with all the humor he could muster, until the girls' giggles filled the room.

Yes, the girls missed his parents, but he'd been a big part of their lives from the beginning. They trusted him to keep them safe. Little did they know he might have no say in the matter, after all.

Chapter Seven

Sarah burned the applesauce, singed the crust of the frozen pumpkin pie and managed to fill the house with smoke twice the morning before Thanksgiving, making her wish Lindsay hadn't needed to grab some holiday groceries.

Renzo hurried in the first time the smoke alarm went off. He charged through the back door like a knight in rancher's coveralls, and when he spotted the pie—and the blackened rim of crust—he tried to wipe away a grin as he scrubbed a hand across his whiskered jaw. "Forgot to set the timer?"

"I think we distracted her," said Kristi. She and Naomi exchanged worried looks. "We're sorry, Aunt Sarah."

"Oh, you sweet thing, you don't have to take the fall for me," Sarah assured her. "It was my fault. But we need pie for tomorrow."

Renzo motioned toward the barn. "Kyle's out there

now, so do you gals mind if I come join you in the kitchen?"

"We would love it if you'd help us in the kitchen!" crowed Chloe as she skipped in from the other room. Her tone of voice didn't exactly dismiss Sarah's contributions, but her preference was quite clear. "Can't we just make a real pie?" she went on. "Like Mama G. does?"

"Lots of ways to make pies," Renzo told her in a firm voice as he ditched his outer work clothes. The temperature was dropping and the wind was picking up, so when he closed the inner door, warmth seemed to encircle them. When he drew closer, smelling of fresh wood and hay and the great outdoors, she realized the warmth might have nothing to do with the door. "And I think Mom has pie dough in the freezer."

He scrubbed his hands in the big sink, then opened the freezer and withdrew a plastic bag. "Success," he told them all with a smile. Then he arched an eyebrow at Sarah and the girls and took a vote. "What kinds of pies do we want?"

"Apple is the best, always!" declared Chloe.

"Not as best as pumpkin," Kristi told her.

"I like pumpkin, too," Naomi added.

"What about you, Sarah?"

He looked over at her, and his gaze lingered. When it did, thoughts of pie and baking flew out the window as other thoughts crept in, and when she tried to shut them down, it didn't work. He drew her. She felt it. Did he?

She thought so at times, but he wasn't an easy read. What good would it do, anyway? His life was here. Hers was hours away in Seattle. This short leave of absence couldn't be extended.

And yet she still found it hard to pull her attention away from him.

"Do you have a favorite?" he asked, and she refocused on the question at hand.

"Pecan," she admitted. "Mom's from Georgia and making pecan pie was always a salute to her roots. And it's just crazy delicious," she added. "But there are three pie crusts there, and you need two for apple and one for pumpkin, I do believe."

"Not if we make a crumb-topped apple," he told her. "Then we have just enough."

She hadn't considered that, but he did, and when he smiled back at her, that warm feeling magnified. "Crumb-topped apple pie is another favorite," she told him, and he grinned.

"Then it's settled. And I know Mom has pecans in the freezer."

"So bugs don't get in them." Naomi pulled up a stool to the counter and took a seat. "Little bugs like to get into nuts in the summer, and Mama G. keeps them in the freezer. Just in case."

"Which should we do first?" Renzo asked the girls as he reached for a pair of mixing bowls in a nearby cupboard.

"Sarah's favorite," said Kristi. "Because that will make it feel special for her."

"Yes!" Naomi fist-pumped the air. "And then we do pumpkin, okay?"

"On it," Renzo told them, and he set the dough

rounds on a plate near the warm stove. "We'll make the fillings, then roll the crusts. That will give them just enough time to thaw."

Sarah was skeptical, but when she realized it took three times as long to include the girls in making the filling, she saw the error of her ways. "You nailed it," she told him as he rolled the first crust out with Naomi's help nearly an hour later. "I didn't think they'd thaw in time."

"When you have so many willing helpers…" His eyes twinkled at her as he let Naomi take a turn with the rolling pin. She went too hard and tore the crust, but he calmly spliced it back together and had her keep going.

When Chloe grew impatient, he reached for two loaves of crusty bread. He broke the loaves in half, set them on the table and put a restaurant-size stainless steel bowl between the hunks of bread. "I need someone to tear this bread into little pieces. Like this," he said, showing them. "Not bigger, okay?"

"I remember!" Kristi scrambled to one of the chairs. "I love this job so much!" She dug right in, tearing the bread with quick motions.

Not Chloe. She frowned and sighed and moved as slowly as she possibly could. Then she said, "Okaaaay," drawing out the word extra-long, in case they didn't realize she was miffed about not doing the first crust. "I know Uncle Kyle likes stuffing, so we should make a lot," she added.

"'Cept he's not coming for Thanksgiving," Kristi told her. "I heard him telling Renzo that they were going someplace else again."

"He doesn't even hardly come to anything anymore," grumbled Chloe. "I bet he won't even come to our birthday party."

"They always come to your birthday party," Renzo replied. "We have to remember that Aunt Valerie has family, too," Renzo continued. "We can't be selfish and expect them to be here all the time, can we?"

"I think if it's a whole family doing Thanksgiving, we can," Naomi noted sensibly. "Or we can just invite Aunt Valerie's family too. We have a very big table," she assured Sarah. "There are extra boards and Renzo can make it like this big." She set the rolling pin down and stretched her arms wide. "I think that will fit lots of people. Don't you?"

She caught the expression on Renzo's face and tried to play peacemaker. "Sometimes we have to do things because of family traditions. My mom's family is far away, so when we go there to visit, we have Thanksgiving dinner, and it can be any time of year. We don't care," she added. "Being together any day is more important than one particular day, isn't it?"

"But if it's a special day, you're supposed to be together. You can't just make stuff up," Chloe told her in a scolding tone of voice. That earned her a reprimand.

"Hey." Renzo leaned around Naomi to catch Chloe's eyes. "Talk nice or don't talk at all. Got it?"

She huffed, rolled her eyes and began tearing at the bread again, but her reaction wasn't lost on Sarah. How could she upset this child's life any more than she already had? Would Chloe come around eventually? Would she adjust to life on the coast if Sarah won custody? Or would she harbor resentment all her life?

"They may look alike, but they're quite unique."

Renzo whispered the words so that Naomi wouldn't hear as she slowly drew the rolling pin across the dough to finish it up.

"I would have thought that impossible." Same DNA. Same appearance, and yet—

"Each with her own soul," he said softly.

His words drew her attention, and there he was, standing right next to her, so close that she could count the tiny points of ivory in his beautiful blue eyes. He met her gaze.

She met his.

And for just a moment she wondered what it would be like to kiss Renzo Calloway. To have those big, strong arms hold her in a warm embrace.

He brought his eyes back up to hers with a look of chagrin on his face. Because he couldn't kiss her here and now? Or because he'd even thought of it?

She thought it was most likely the latter when he shoulder-bumped her lightly. When she looked up, the twinkle in his eyes set her pulse thrumming all over again.

Then he took the rolling pin from Naomi's hand, put it into Sarah's and took a place next to her. "Let's see what you've got, Doc. I'll help." He showed her how to position the rolling pin onto the dough, then slowly wind it up and place it gently in the pie pan.

It tore almost in half. She screeched softly, but Renzo lifted the torn half, set it into the pan so it slightly overlapped the other half and slipped it back to her. "Just press it together along the seam. Once it's baked, it will be fine. It happens all the time."

She did that, and then he stepped closer. Close enough that she could breathe in the scent of him, fresh air, a woodsy soap and sweet pie filling. A heady combination, all told.

"Now we fold and crimp, which is not my strong suit," he told her. "You've got smaller hands. If I show you how, can you help Naomi while Chloe and I roll the next crust?"

"Sure." He demonstrated the pinch-crimp to her.

"Got it." She picked up the pie plate and moved to the table, making room for Chloe at the counter. It took another hour before the pies were actually in the oven, one in the top oven and two down below.

"Different temperatures," he explained, when he programmed the ovens. "Fruit pies need a higher temperature than custard pies."

"We can clean up while they bake," she replied.

"Can we watch a show?" asked Kristi. She yawned and stretched after she spoke. "The princess one?"

"You guys have earned it," Renzo told her. "I'll turn it on." Just then, his phone buzzed. He read the text and frowned. "I've got to head to the barn. I don't mean to leave you with all of this." He indicated the messy counters and tabletop.

"You were here for the creative side," she assured him. "When I said I don't cook, I meant it, but I'm masterful at cleanup. And my mother should be back from the store any minute."

"I believe I've mentioned my kitchen prowess before, Sarah." He said it softly, as if one of them knowing how to cook was enough.

It wasn't, and she couldn't let the rugged cop draw her off course. "Between you and Mom, we'll have the holiday covered with no problem," she replied, but she didn't look up. "See you later."

He turned on the show for the girls and tugged on his ranch clothes. "Back soon," he called.

She wanted to look up. Meet his gaze. Exchange a smile.

She didn't. She kept facing the sink as she rinsed dishes. "All right."

When the door clicked shut behind him, the room felt emptier. Cooler. He exuded a presence. The protector in him, she supposed, and when the door opened a few moments later, she turned. "Forget something?"

But it wasn't Renzo coming into the kitchen.

It was Valerie.

She took one look at Sarah, sat down and promptly burst into tears.

And these weren't just any tears. Sarah sensed that right off. These were the tears of a broken heart, so she crossed the room, took the seat alongside Valerie and quietly covered the other woman's hands with her own. And then—silently—she prayed.

"I blew the hydraulic lines," Kyle muttered when Renzo came into the barn. "I tried to do too much, too soon, and the whole thing erupted."

It sure had. Renzo couldn't even imagine what his brother had done to blow two lines out.

He wanted to berate him. Frankly, he'd been wanting to do that for a while, but one look at the agony on his brother's face made him shift tactics. "They're just hoses, Kyle. Nothing we can't fix."

Kyle stared at him.

Because he was being nice? Or was there something else going on?

Then his brother nodded. "Just hoses. Yeah. Something we can fix." He aimed a work light toward the hydraulic framework. "We'll have to get new ones."

"Let's head to the supply store. They're still open, and Sarah's with the girls. Although the pies are in the oven, so I'm taking a big chance here," he joked, trying to ease the tension, then texted Sarah.

She sent back a thumbs-up emoji. Won't burn pies. Promise. Timer is set.

"We're good," he told Kyle. They climbed into Renzo's pickup truck and he drove toward Quincy. It wasn't a long drive, but the thick silence made it feel long. They obtained the hoses and new clamps and couplers, then headed back to the ranch, still quiet.

Renzo turned the radio on. The cab filled instantly with lilting tunes of kid music. The girls' CDs were filled with childhood favorites and a few of his, too, but he was pretty sure Kyle didn't need this right now. He moved to change the music.

Kyle stopped him. "It's all right. Better than Christmas," he said gruffly, and Renzo grimaced. He loved Christmas music. He loved everything about Christmas. He got a kick out of prepping for the holiday with the girls and his mother. Being silly and reverent, all at once, because he never forgot the reason for the season.

But he'd read the sorrow in his brother's eyes, and he wasn't about to argue with him. Whatever was going on with Kyle wasn't going to be solved by arguing about Christmas music. He pulled up alongside the barn.

Kyle climbed out. He grabbed the box of hoses and accessories and headed toward the barn. "I've got this. You go back and take care of the kids."

Yesterday Renzo would have been tempted to do just that, and as a cold north wind gusted into his face, he was somewhat tempted now. But he'd seen the grief in his brother's eyes, and no matter how much of a bonehead Kyle had been, he couldn't. He shut the driver's door and followed Kyle into the barn. "It'll go a lot quicker with two of us, and there's still time to make more pies if Sarah's burned the ones we just made."

A photo text came through right then, a shot of three pies, cooling on the counter, and not one of them was burned. He grinned, then held up the picture for Kyle. "Pies are safe. I'm all yours."

Kyle almost smiled. Then his expression faded once more. "She seems nice."

"She is. Real nice. And smart. And her mother's wonderful, and she's got a great job so if she goes for custody of the girls, I can't imagine a judge wanting to refuse her," Renzo admitted.

"But Jenn left custody to Mom and Dad." Kyle frowned as he worked to remove the blown hoses. "How can she fight her sister's wishes?" he asked, then sighed.

"Oh, right." He answered his own question. "Jenn didn't know she existed, and that could have made a big difference."

"Exactly."

"I hate life sometimes."

Renzo's ears perked up.

"Not the living part, but all the things you can't control," Kyle told him as he retrained a light onto the tractor's hydraulics. "We make all the right choices, do all the right things, and it gets messed up anyway. And there's nothing you can do about it. The ranch. Dad. The weather. Everything," he muttered as he worked the first hose free.

Renzo was generally good at explaining to Kyle how wrong he was about things.

Not today. Kyle's sadness worried him, and as he worked to attach the new right-hand line, he bit his tongue. Not because he wanted to, but because it seemed like the right thing to do.

"Is that clamp working?"

Renzo recognized the change of subject as he tightened the screw firmly. "Nice and snug."

Kyle grunted. The sound of tires on the driveway drew his head up. He paused, as if he could see through the barn walls, and when the car's lights headed west, toward his house, he sighed.

And then, chin down, he got back to work while Renzo silently prayed for his brother, for Valerie and for whatever was going on in Kyle's head, because while Kyle wasn't the most ambitious person in the world, he was never despondent.

Today he was, and Renzo wasn't sure what that meant for the ranch and the legacy of Calloway Beef, but under the current circumstances, it didn't bode well.

Chapter Eight

Sarah heard the back door open a little past six. So did the girls. They raced for the door. They didn't see the tired look in Renzo's eyes, or the initial stoop of his shoulders as he stepped into the enclosed porch.

Sarah did.

He replaced the look with a quick smile when the girls attacked him, then shooed them off momentarily. "Nasty clothes," he told them. "We were doing some tractor maintenance and I'm pretty messed up. Let me shed the outer layers, okay?"

"Yes, but we have such good news!" shouted Chloe, never one to be outdone. "We have three, count them one-two-three." She used her fingers to illustrate her very important message. "Unburned pies and they smell so good! I don't even know why we can't have some pie tonight because remember how Aunt Sarah said it's not about the day, like you can celebrate any day. Right, Aunt Sarah?"

"Little did I know my wonderful words would come

back to haunt me so quickly," she told Chloe. "We have the cookies you made with my mom for a treat tonight, remember? Let's save the pies for tomorrow. Part of the fun is the anticipation, right?"

"I've been 'ticipating all day because they smell so good," grumbled Chloe, but then she brightened right back up. "Except I love cookies, too, and maybe with ice cream on them? Like a special treat for helping get ready?"

"Did you eat your carrots?" Sarah pointed to the single plate on the counter. "I do believe veggies are crucial for growth. Right?"

"Except I hate carrots," Chloe muttered, but when she spotted the container of cookies on the counter, she huffed her way over to the table. "But I'll eat them. Not because you're making me." She made sure that Sarah understood her reasoning. "Because it would make Mama G. sad if I don't follow directions. And I don't ever want to make Mama G. sad."

What could Sarah say to that? She shifted her attention back to Kristi and Naomi and Renzo.

He'd kicked his coveralls aside when the girls retackled him, and when he tried to reach down to retrieve them, she stepped in. "You go enjoy the girls. I'll throw these in. I've actually figured out this washing machine. I can't say we're friends," she stressed, smiling. "But we are no longer mortal enemies."

"It's a start." He smiled down at her.

She smiled back, and there it was again, that connection. The attraction. Did he feel it too? And if he did, did he realize how impossible it all was?

Or the best solution ever.

She broke the connection reluctantly. It wasn't that she disliked happy endings. She loved them. Seeing a family go home with a healthy baby was her constant goal, but it didn't always end up that way. And in her heart she owed it to Jenn to make this right, but was that what she was doing? Or could she be making things wrong out of her own sense of justice?

"Was Valerie over here?"

It wasn't a casual question, but how could she answer it? She'd been sworn to secrecy by a grieving woman struggling with the roller coaster of infertility treatments that hadn't gone well so far. For whatever reason, probably because Gina wasn't available, she'd become a much-needed shoulder that afternoon. "She stopped by and we had coffee. Well, I had coffee. She had water."

He sent the girls off to the living room. Chloe had finished her carrots. She set her plate near the sink and skipped off to join her sisters. "Did Valerie seem all right?" he asked softly.

She hesitated purposely. She'd promised to keep Valerie's medical issues to herself, but he was clearly asking for a reason. "No. She's struggling, but I can't say more than that, all right?"

His face shadowed. He stared out the window. The dusk-to-dawn light bathed the graveled driveway in pale yellow light. Beyond that, Kyle's truck sat parked outside the barn, well past time for him to have normally gone home.

Renzo looked from his brother's truck, back to her. "They're both in a rough place," he admitted. "I don't know why. Kyle isn't exactly a talker. But I've watched several deputies go through broken marriages."

He thought their marriage was in trouble, a reasonable assumption on his part, and she couldn't confirm or deny it. That made her feel like a liar.

"I don't know how to help. I don't know if there's any way an outsider can help," he admitted.

Kyle stepped out of the barn just then. He didn't look their way. He barely looked up. Chin down, he moved to his truck, as if the last place he wanted to go was home. He got into the truck, started the engine and headed toward the road.

Renzo watched him go, then turned and folded his arms. "But I know what has to be done here to help my parents through this rough time. They need the girls loved and the ranch running smoothly, but once my leave is up, how can I help with all of that while I'm working?" He put up a hand. "You don't have to answer. It's a rhetorical question. I know I can't. No one person could. It will crush my mother if we lose the girls, and it will crush my father if we lose the ranch. I don't want to make either choice, but Kyle's head isn't in the game and once I'm back to work, there won't be time to dig him out of trouble. What then?"

Her mother bustled through the side porch door just then. Sarah seized the interruption to save herself from tackling a question with no answers. "Temperature's dropping," Lindsay said as she came into the kitchen. She spotted the pies on the counter and didn't hide her surprise. "Sarah, you outdid yourself, those pies are marvelous. I'm impressed."

"I had some expert advice," she told her mother with a glance toward Renzo. "The initial pie was an utter failure. Then reenforcements stepped in and helped me see the error of my ways."

"And we helped!" Kristi slid into the room on sock-clad feet. "See how slippery this floor is? I love it!"

"It's a great sliding floor," noted Lindsay. She smiled down at Kristi and palmed her head. "Thank you for helping with the pies. And who broke up all that stuffing bread?" she asked.

"Us." Kristi leaned into Lindsay's touch as if she belonged there. The sweetness of the moment gripped Sarah.

Then Kristi stepped away and faced Renzo. "We're going to see Grandpa tomorrow, aren't we? We always go see him on special days."

"And other days," he reminded her, but he nodded. "First thing in the morning. We can't stay long. Miss Mortie says he gets tired real quick these days." He shifted his attention back to Sarah. "Carol Mortimer oversees a lot of in-home patient care in Golden Grove. Mr. Drew was part of her caseload before he was moved to assisted living two years ago."

"And now he's in skilled care?" She understood the importance of those terms. The girls' grandfather was failing. How would they handle losing him on top of everything else?

"We'll be so good," Kristi promised.

Renzo looked skeptical as she hurried off to tell the others. "She means well, but she's making promises she can't keep," he noted. "Naomi gets emotional when she visits her grandfather, and Chloe never wants to leave. His growing weakness bothers her. For a tough cookie, she's got a caregiver's heart."

"Another similarity between Chloe and Sarah," Lindsay noted. "Funny how things pass down, isn't it?"

"The intricacies of DNA amaze me," Sarah replied. "More so now that I've met my nieces."

"I need to clean up." Renzo crossed the room. He still looked tired, but not defeated. Square-shouldered, he seemed determined to balance what couldn't be balanced and she understood the dilemma. How would she choreograph work, the girls' schedules, a nanny, a new place to live with room enough for the triplets, and the fact that her parents were across the Sound on an island? Lovely to visit, but not exactly conducive to emergency help if needed. And if she was awarded custody, could she take the girls back to Seattle and not visit their sick grandfather? Of course not. Heart heavy, she bit her lip.

Lindsay looped an arm around Sarah's shoulders. "Your conundrum is twofold," she told her in a soft voice. "Saving preemies means constantly monitoring every tiny detail that might throw you a curve," she continued. "It's an amazing feat, but life isn't like that, my love." She leaned her head against Sarah's briefly. "Life is full of twists and turns we can't anticipate, and sometimes we just have to take the ride and see where they lead. There's no way to plan for every possible outcome. That's why it's good to keep the Serenity Prayer close at hand."

The prayer talked about acceptance and courage and wisdom. Three important aspects of life. "I try to remind myself of that, but you know I don't like giving up control."

"I expect that's part of what's fueling your reaction, honey," her mother said softly. "You've got three identical girls in the other room, but that's in looks only. Think of how each of them would react to any given situation, and you can see the problem you're facing. Maybe it's time to let go and let God," Lindsay advised. "Highly intelligent people often think they've got complete control over their destiny. They don't. Sometimes the smarter you are, the tougher that is to accept."

Sarah's visit with Valerie exemplified that. As an accomplished corporate executive for one of the Washington fruit conglomerates, the well-educated woman was stymied by what should be easy—the ability to conceive and carry a child. Her education had landed her a great job, but nature had thwarted her on a very basic level. "You make a great point."

Lindsay squeezed her shoulder lightly. "I generally do. You and your dad love being in charge. It's not always possible in real life and that's hard to accept. Not only for you, but for our detective friend, too."

Renzo's life had been flipped upside down in multiple ways the day she arrived.

And yet he hadn't fallen apart. He'd soldiered on, not only dealing with the situation, but inviting her into their home. Their lives. How many people would do that willingly?

Pretty much no one she knew, and she wondered what that said about her. She'd always purposely insulated herself from drama. Maybe from life. Was that because she dealt with life-and-death decisions daily at the NICU? Or was it self-protection?

"I'm going to read the girls a story." Lindsay moved toward the broad family room, but on the way she stopped to smell the pies. Then she looked back at Sarah. "If nothing else, you two made a great team today."

"They're just pies, Mom."

"Everything begins somewhere, darling." She winked. "Why not here? Why not now?"

She knew the reasons why not, but when Renzo came down the stairs a few minutes later, her resolve thinned.

He noted Lindsay and the girls, then crossed to Sarah's side. "I'm going to get everything chopped up for the stuffing. Then we'll put it together when we get back from the nursing home tomorrow. Do you want to come, Sarah?" he asked. "Jenn's dad knows about you. I don't know how much he'll remember from our conversation, but I stopped by the other day and brought him up to speed."

"Should I?" She turned and leaned her back against the countertop while he set celery and onion and apples next to the cutting board. "I don't want to upset him."

He directed his full attention to her and held her gaze.

Instant trouble, because she wanted to go on gazing up at him. Watching the pale points of light in his sky blue eyes brighten with sincerity. When Renzo Calloway locked eyes with her, she never had to wonder if his attention was wandering. It wasn't. The guy focused 100 percent on her, and that simple fact spiked her pulse.

"Your presence wouldn't upset him. What the agency did *was* upsetting," he stressed. "Separating you and Jenn without giving either family a chance to take you both was a horrible decision, but Lanny was a victim, too. And it honestly might give him comfort to meet you," he added. "He doted on Jenn. She meant the world to him." His voice deepened. "He was older when they adopted Jenn, and he was there at everything she did, before and after his wife died. Jenn was his world, and when he got sick, she was there for him, too. I think his illness was part of why she decided to start a family."

"Decided?" Sarah frowned. They'd never talked about why the girls had no father of record.

"The girls were planned," he told her, and she lifted her brows in surprise. "Jenn was smart but not always patient, and she got tired of waiting for Mr. Right. She said she'd dealt with far too many Mr. Wrongs and she wanted to have a family, so why not be a single mom?" He frowned as he worked on the celery. "She was making decent money as a PA in Wenatchee. No one expected triplets. And no one dreamed what might happen, but here we are. When she found out she was carrying three babies, she drew up her will. Jenn liked being prepared."

Something else they had in common.

"Things went bad at week thirty-three. By week thirty-four they had to deliver the girls." He'd picked up the knife to begin chopping, then didn't. He sighed and set the knife aside. "But then Jenn didn't make it."

"Eclampsia."

Grim, he nodded. "Yes. Then she was gone."

"And she'd listed your family as guardians for the girls."

He nodded. "She understood her father's prognosis, so she asked us about guardianship before she'd had the will done. We said yes."

Her older sister had dotted her i's and crossed her t's to ensure her children's future, so what right did Sarah have to mess that all up? She'd come to Golden Grove thinking she had every right. Now she wasn't so sure. "She was thorough."

"Always. And she loved medicine. Funny how that worked out, isn't it? That you both went into medicine?" He picked up the knife again and began slicing the celery into long, thin spears. "Not all siblings are alike."

Was he thinking of himself and Kyle?

She withdrew another knife from the drawer. "I'll do the apples, okay? Onions make me cry."

"Deal." He handed the big peach-toned apple to her.

Her hand closed over the apple. And over his hand.

He looked down at their joined hands. Then he drew his eyes up to hers slowly, as if wondering. His eyes asked a question. A question she longed to answer with a chorus of yeses.

She swallowed hard.

He noticed. And then he smiled.

Oh, that smile!

It didn't tempt her, it pulled her in, full force, like a storm wind racing across the Sound.

"Renzo! You would love this cartoon so much. It's got a whole bunch of kids making popcorn for Thanksgiving and they don't even have one little bit of turkey!"

Naomi's lilting voice brought her to her senses. She pulled back, accepted the apple, then waved it at him. "Do not flirt with me," she said in a scolding whisper. "Flirting is unacceptable under our terms and conditions."

"Sarah." He waited until she glanced up. "We have no terms and conditions. We're making this up as we go." He sent her a quick glance of genuine regret. "We also have no clue what the coming months are going to bring, but I'm sure of two things. You have to get back to saving lives in Seattle, and I've got to make sure everything stays solid here, with three children's futures that lie in the balance. In thirty-eight years I've never let my parents down. There's no way I can break that streak now. If things were different—"

"But they're not," she told him firmly. "We need to put the girls first. I thought I knew what that meant when I came here. Now I'm second-guessing myself. And we're surrounded by uncertainties." His father and the girls' grandfather were both in dire straits, so how could she tip the score to her advantage and live with herself?

But they that wait upon the Lord shall renew their strength; they shall mount up with wings as eagles; they shall run, and not be weary; they shall walk, and not faint. The beautiful quote from Isaiah had guided her through grueling years of med school and training. She'd had to learn patience and humility to face the rigors of the NICU. "Whatever this is—" she waved a hand between them, and refused to get caught up in his little smile "—we can't let it get in the way, Renzo."

"I know." His smile faded, and she hated that he agreed with her. "For now, let's just do the best we can for the holidays. The chance to give the girls the true spirit of Christmas over the next few weeks, like my mom would do if she were here. Deal?"

She took a deep breath, then shoulder-bumped him lightly. "Deal."

Chapter Nine

Renzo took a picture of the girls and sent it to his mother on Thanksgiving morning. On our way to visit Lanny. Then back home to prepare the feast!

Wonderful! she texted back. Renzo, thank you so much for taking charge of all this. I know you hate taking time off. Don't think I don't appreciate the sacrifice you're making.

All good, he texted her, but her words gave him food for thought. It was true, he didn't like taking time off.

Was he a workaholic?

Kind of.

He enjoyed his days off, but he'd been known to take overtime shifts weekly to fill the department's needs.

His mother cautioned him about it regularly.

He laughed it off because he loved his work. He was born to be a protector, watching out for others. It suited him. And he'd done his share of dating, but he'd never been really tempted to be more than casual.

Until now. Didn't it figure that Sarah Brown would be the one, and at the worst possible time?

He parked the SUV in the small parking lot and hit the unlock button. The girls spilled out as Sarah parked two spots down. She'd chosen to drive separately. She used holiday preparations as an excuse, but he sensed her nervousness about meeting Jenn's adoptive father. Having her own car gave her the option to leave whenever she wanted.

The girls hurried up the sidewalk, carrying construction paper cards while he held a beautiful bouquet of flowers Sarah had ordered for the nursing facility.

Thoughtful.

Kind.

Beautiful.

She drew her scarf around her neck and came closer to him. "It smells like snow." She was picking a safe topic to chat about. He played along, glancing toward the clouds.

"It won't stick yet, but it's definitely in the air." She'd fallen into step with him, but when he reached for the door, she hesitated. He paused and looked down. "You okay?"

"I don't want to upset him."

"You won't."

"You can't know that." She drew her eyebrows together.

He conceded with a slight shrug. "All he ever wanted was the best for his daughter. Losing his wife was rough, but then losing Jenn hit him hard. I think discovering that the girls have a biological relative actually pleased him. He tires easy, so we won't stay long."

She preceded him into the lobby. The girls had surrounded a wheelchair-bound man in a bright, cozy room on their right. Several elderly patients were in the solarium-style sitting area. A couple were playing checkers. Two others were watching the Thanksgiving Day parade on TV, but having the girls descend tended to disrupt any gathering.

The old women exclaimed over them. The men paused their game and laughed at the noisy threesome. Only one aged man scowled at the noisy interruption. He stood up, slapped his newspaper against his leg and shuffled off with his walker, muttering.

Renzo moved forward to make sure the girls didn't totally overwhelm Lanny. Kristi giggled and stepped to one side.

So did Naomi.

And then Lanny spotted Sarah.

His eyes went wide. His breath caught. He stared, then tried to reach out, but his wasting muscles refused to obey. "My dear." He whispered the words in a voice that dripped emotion. "You're Sarah?"

She crossed the last few feet and knelt alongside his chair. "Yes."

He lay his hands atop hers. His eyes closed briefly, and for a moment Renzo wondered if Sarah had been right in hesitating. Maybe seeing her was too much for Jenn's dad.

Then he opened his eyes.

Joy brightened them. Mixed with something else,

something poignant. He kept his hands on hers as he studied her face, her features, her hair, and then he sighed. "You're so much like her, but you're your own person, too, aren't you?"

"I'd like to think so. I've had a good life," she told him.

"So did Jenn," he replied softly. "We made sure of it. Lord have mercy, we loved that girl and it was such a blessing to get her. When the agency called and said they had a little girl, not quite two years old, we were ecstatic. But if we'd known about you, Sarah…" He had to pause a moment to catch his breath, and the oxygen tank that fed his nose tube made a noise. "Sorry." He frowned, frustrated by the lack of air and muscle weakness his body endured. "We would have loved both of you. I hope you know that. We would have never chosen one when we could have had two. Just so you know."

The effort to talk left him breathless.

Once his breathing calmed, Sarah didn't hold back. She leaned in, reached out and held him.

Lanny's eyes filled with tears.

He tried to blink them back, but that only made them slip down his weathered cheeks.

Renzo grabbed a couple of tissues and gently blotted the tears away.

"Why is Grandpa crying?" Chloe glared up at him, then Sarah. "Why did you make him cry?" she demanded. She crossed her arms and scowled.

"Because we're happy to see each other, dear."

Chloe's frown suggested otherwise.

"And because we both miss your mom."

"You didn't know our mom." When Chloe rolled her eyes, Naomi smacked her on the arm.

"I knew you when you were a baby," Naomi argued.

"Well, we were born together," Chloe replied.

"But Sarah knew our mom for months, so she did know her, Chloe."

Kristi took Naomi's side. "She knew her when she was little, and you never, ever, ever forget a sister. Like ever."

Chloe stared at Kristi, then Naomi, and then she did something she rarely did. She backed down. "I didn't think of that, I guess."

"I was almost seven months old when the Browns adopted me, so your mom and I were together that long. And I think somewhere, in the back of my mind, I always wondered about my family," Sarah told them. "But it wasn't until recently that people could check it out. It just didn't happen quite in time for your mom and me to meet. But I get to meet you guys. And all kinds of nice people here. That's a pretty special thing to celebrate on Thanksgiving, I think."

"A reason to be grateful," agreed Lanny. He sighed then. Renzo noticed the sign of fatigue. So did Sarah. She stood. "I'd like to come visit again, if it's all right with you, sir."

"I would love that." His voice rasped and she stepped back.

"I'll head back to the house now and help Mom and Dad."

Renzo nodded. Sarah was stepping back to give the girls some time alone with Lanny, but there was no mistaking the raw emotion on her face, and when she swiped a tissue to her eyes on her way out the door, Renzo's heart went tight.

The injustice gripped him. He excelled at unraveling puzzles, setting things right, helping to secure evidence and build cases against wrongdoers, but there was no way to fix a decades-old mistake like this.

The front desk receptionist moved their way. "Anyone want one of these?" she asked. She proffered three bright-toned turkey-shaped lollipops.

"Oh, thank you!" Kristi and Naomi dashed her way. "These are so cute!" Naomi exclaimed.

"I remember you gave us these last year, too," Kristi told her, and the woman nodded.

"I order some every year for our holiday visitors," she told them.

"I'm always sad when I have some left over at the end of the day," she said to Renzo.

He knew what she meant. Not everyone in the facility had family that came to see them.

Chloe stayed by Lanny's side. Naomi brought a lollipop to her. "I got one for you."

"Thanks."

Renzo cleared his throat softly.

Chloe knew what that meant. It was their quiet signal that it was almost time to go. She gulped and clung to her grandfather's hand. "A little longer? Please?"

"Two minutes," he told her softly.

She swallowed hard, then nodded before she leaned close. She didn't say anything. Renzo was pretty sure she couldn't. She simply laid her head against her grandfather's chest and arm and stayed there, eyes closed.

The two old ladies had drawn Kristi's and Naomi's attention as they fussed over their cute outfits, but Chloe stayed tucked along the curve of her grandfather's arm. Renzo didn't want to end the moment, but Lanny's strength was fading. When he reached down and gently touched Chloe's arm, she sighed. Then she opened her eyes and whispered just loud enough for Renzo and Lanny to hear. "I love you, Grandpa. So much."

Lanny lifted his hand to her head. He set it there for just a moment, but weakness prevailed and his hand slipped to his lap of its own volition. He sighed. "I love you, too, Chloe. All three of you."

"Girls?" Renzo motioned Kristi and Naomi over. "Time to say goodbye. We'll come back again on Saturday."

"Love you, Grandpa!" Kristi gave him a gentle hug, but not gentle enough. Lanny winced, but didn't make a sound.

Naomi didn't hug. She set her hand on his arm, leaned close and fluttered her eyelashes against his cheek. "Butterfly kisses," she whispered to him. "Butterfly kisses are the lightest ones ever. They don't hurt at all, do they, Grandpa?"

He smiled slightly. Muscle weakness made everything difficult for him, even showing emotion.

Chloe lifted her head. She planted a gentle kiss on his other cheek and stood. "Love you, Gramps. See you soon!"

His tiny smile deepened slightly before fading, but

it was enough for Chloe. She stepped back and reached for Renzo's hand. She didn't do that as often as the other girls. Today her tight grip said more than words.

Naomi and Kristi skipped ahead, less aware of the seriousness of Lanny's condition.

But Chloe clung to his hand, and when she stepped outside, she paused, much like Sarah had done. She glanced around. Glanced back. Then took a deep breath and walked slowly to the SUV.

"That was an amazing meal, Lindsay." Renzo lifted the pictures he'd sent to his printer and slipped them into a padded envelope. "And Sarah, Mom will love the pics. And she and Aunt Shelly will both love the pie."

"Can Grandpa have pie?" asked Kristi. "Maybe we should send more, right?"

"Grandpa can't chew things yet," Renzo told her. "We can make more pies for Christmas, okay? Or whenever. As soon as Grandpa can eat regular stuff, we'll bring him all of his favorites."

"Not liver," announced Chloe. "I do not want to help make liver. It's awful."

"But Papa loves it," Naomi replied. "So maybe it's just good for him. But not me," she added quickly, in case anyone thought otherwise.

"We'll take care of the liver," Renzo assured them. He slipped the envelope into his coat pocket. "I will give them your love, your cards, the pictures and pie. That's a good Thanksgiving visit." He turned toward Sarah and her parents. "Thank you for helping put this all together. I liked helping Mom do things, but I can't say I really understood all the steps it takes to pull off a holiday like this. Now I do, and my appreciation has increased exponentially."

"I feel the same way." Sarah motioned to the soft hum of the dishwasher. "And we're blessed to have amazing machines that help. It had to be tough in the pre-dishwasher days, right?"

"Families helped each other," Lindsay told them. "People didn't just stay with their own families like this. They'd gather together and share the feast and the work."

"Like a potluck," Kevin, Sarah's father, added. "My grandparents used to organize the community Thanksgiving for their hometown in Kentucky. There were maybe fifty families or more. Kids of all ages. Parents. Grandparents. A real old-fashioned gathering. I don't know if they still do that, but I've never forgotten those celebrations."

"It makes it a shared experience," Lindsay added. "Is your brother going with you?"

Renzo nodded as the side door opened and Kyle came in. "Yes. I'll see you guys tomorrow, okay?"

The girls mobbed him. He hugged each one, assured them that he had their new cards for Grandpa and stood. He made eye contact with Sarah and her parents. "Thank you again. I can't say more than that."

"I'm glad to get the chance to spend a little time with these three," Kevin Brown told him.

"Drive safe," added Lindsay.

Sarah had gone over to the coffee maker. She turned, crossed the room and thrust a to-go cup of coffee at him. She didn't want to worry about him making the long drive in the rain after eating a big meal, and coffee was her go-to in times of stress.

"Thank you, Sarah." He accepted the coffee and took a sip, then smiled at her. Just her. "Perfect."

The smile suggested he wasn't simply referring to the hot drink. She ignored him on purpose. "Turkey can make you sleepy, and it's a long drive to the coast in the rain." Clouds had darkened the afternoon sky, and the rain had begun in earnest a few minutes before.

"We'll take turns," Kyle assured her. "But coffee's not a bad idea."

She poured him a cup, too, and after Kyle had added a dash of cream, the two men left.

Her parents stayed and played games with the girls. By the time they left, the triplets were worn out. She tucked them into bed and came back downstairs to a quiet house.

Silence surrounded her. It felt strange to be alone in the Calloway house on a holiday. She glanced around, feeling out of place even though this family had gone out of their way to make her feel welcome and better yet, needed. Was she truly a help or an interloper, wanting her way?

The side door swung open just then. Renzo came in. He turned to shut the door and the set of his shoulders drew her sympathy. She moved his way, and when he saw her, he smiled as if seeing her was enough to make things better. Sarah couldn't remember seeing that kind of reaction from any of her old suitors. But from Renzo, it seemed to come naturally. "It's quiet."

She laughed softly. "I was noticing that, too. Too quiet. It felt strange."

"Well, there hasn't been much quiet time since you arrived, and there won't be much going forward, so we should bask in it for the moment," he said as he moved forward.

"How was Seattle? Your mom? Your mom and dad?" She spoke softly as he slung his jacket over the back of a chair near the fireplace He took that chair while she settled into one across from him. "Unless you'd rather not talk about it."

He hesitated slightly before he replied. "Not talking isn't going to change anything, is it?"

She shook her head. "No."

He leaned forward, folded his hands and took a moment. "I don't see much improvement, Sarah. Little, if any. And he looks so desperately unhappy. Almost as if—"

"He wishes we hadn't saved him."

He didn't respond, but his expression agreed.

"Renzo, I'm so sorry."

He grimaced. "They said it might take months for his brain to heal and even longer for him to make substantial progress. They're talking about a long-term nursing facility, and I don't even know what to say about that, because the last thing my father would want is long-term care. The guy wrote a DNR years ago. My mother knew about it, but they hadn't mentioned it to me or Kyle. She said Dad was so against nursing homes that he insisted on drawing it up when they were still in their fifties. He didn't want her to say anything, said he didn't want us to try and talk him out of it, and Mom said she went along because the chances of it being needed were slim. She didn't want to argue with him, so now he feels like she betrayed him. He can't talk, but he's clearly angry with her."

"Oh, Renzo. I'm so sorry."

"Except that I wouldn't change a thing, Sarah, and what does that say about me?" he asked. "If I had known, I would have still done life-saving measures even if you weren't here to help, because no one knows the outcome of something like this. Why would we ever shrug off life? So it's not on you, because I'd have done the same thing. But it's hard to see him wishing we'd all just stepped back."

"I don't think I could have," she told him. "Instinct kicks in and you jump into action. It's not like he had a terminal illness or something."

"Exactly. And I wanted to scold him, but how do you scold someone for not wanting pain and suffering?" He sighed, and clenched his hands. "They suggested the same nursing facility that Lanny's in because it's close to the house."

That advice startled her. "But that's not a rehab facility. It's a skilled nursing home." It wasn't Sarah's call to make, but the thought of tucking Renzo's father into a home for the aged seemed wrong. "What's the prognosis?"

"Uncertain."

"That means a possible recovery," she told him.

He frowned. "He can't eat. He can't move. He can't function. I don't see how—"

"Hear me out." She'd taken the seat across from him, but this was too important a discussion, so she picked up a footstool and went to sit in front of him. "I understand that he may have irreversible brain damage. It's hard to know, even with scans because the brain takes a long time to heal, but it's crucial to get him the physical therapy he needs right now. That avoids atrophied muscles, and helps keep the connection between brain and muscles intact. When my grandfather suffered a stroke, it was a long road back, but he did come back, Renzo. And we had the chance to have him with us for twelve more years, and he was ten years older than your dad. I've seen amazing things happen. With the right care and motivation."

"He can barely move, Sarah."

"That's true right now." She gave him a frank look. "But that's because the damage is fresh. I understand the conundrum you're facing, because no one wants to go against a parent's wishes and this puts your mother in a horrible spot."

"She's the eternal optimist married to a dyed-in-the-wool realist, so she's caught in the middle. Mom always says with life, there's hope, but she'd promised him that she'd never put him in a home. He wanted to die with his boots on. He said that often enough. Yet here we are."

"Cowboy rugged." She reached out and took his hands in hers. "But if he gets put into therapy ASAP, then you're giving him the best chance of coming out of this. There are no guarantees, but if he goes to a home with no physical therapy program in place, you're basically signing his death certificate."

"So why wouldn't they just send him to one of those?" Renzo asked.

Sarah was pretty sure she knew why. "I expect they're getting mixed signals. From him, from your mom and then the fact that he didn't want to be resuscitated and didn't want long-term care weighs in. If he's got no fight left in him, then it's a tough call to make."

"Maybe some battles are too big to take on." She frowned and he acknowledged her expression quickly. "You think he's got a chance?"

"I don't know," she told him honestly. "And I don't want to be responsible for pushing you in a direction that doesn't work, but if your dad is willing to fight and we can increase his mobility once his heart is strong enough, it's amazing what the body can do to heal itself. He's already defied the odds," she reminded him. "It's rare for people to live through the combination of ischemic stroke and cardiac arrest. Your dad did it. Now you need to clear the path for the rest of his recovery, and a lot of that depends on good heart health and mobility."

"I suppose the best facilities for that are in Seattle or Spokane, correct?"

She squeezed his hand lightly. "There are good ones there to get him started, but you've got a really good one right over in Ellensburg. Top-rated, great programs and solid results. I checked out ratings after I saw your dad on that video. That stubborn look told me he was just plain mad that he's in the predicament he'd always feared, so now the question is, does he have the strength and will to pull himself up and out?"

"I've never known a stronger man," Renzo replied.

"That might be true, but you have to go into this knowing the results aren't guaranteed," she cautioned him. "Right now he's at the base of the mountain, and the climb looks formidable. But most climbs get better when we get near the top. Here's the thing, though." She locked eyes with him and inched slightly closer. "It's hard work. He'll get mad. He'll get discouraged. He'll want to quit. But if the cowboy I met here has your kind of gumption, he's got a shot at doing this, Renzo, and I'd be wrong to say otherwise. But there's honestly no time to waste because if he's not cooperating with them—"

"And my mom doesn't have the heart to push him."

"Exactly. But I expect you and Kyle can urge him back on the right track. Something to think about, anyway." She stood and tapped her watch. "Gotta go. It's getting late."

He stood, too. "Sarah?"

She met his gaze. "Yes?"

He reached for her, and this time she didn't step back. He pulled her into a hug. A beautiful, wonderful hug. His arms didn't just embrace her, they encompassed her, as if she was meant to be here, in this man's arms, forever.

You could work in Golden Grove. Or he could work in Seattle. Why complicate this?

Because it wasn't that simple. Her skill levels demanded a highly trained facility with intricate equipment that wasn't found at every hospital. And he was caught in the middle of a major family crisis here.

But when he dropped his cheek to her hair, she didn't

want to think about the variables. In the end, she had no choice. If things were different, maybe they could bridge that gap, but right now, it was next to impossible. The last thing she wanted to do was end this embrace, but she did it. "Thank you for that," she told him, moving back.

He didn't let go. He simply loosened his arms. "I like holding you, Sarah."

She started to speak, but he quieted her when he leaned his forehead against hers. "You don't have to say anything. I get it, but I want you to know that for all the tough things that have gone on these past few weeks, your presence has become a cornerstone for all of us, so maybe this is part of a plan. Maybe this isn't an accident of timing because of someone's horrible decision-making. Maybe, somehow, this was meant to be."

"Destiny?" She wasn't about to buy into that notion. "It's a pretty convoluted route, don't you think?"

"Wasn't it William Cowper who said the Lord works in mysterious ways?"

She couldn't excuse the past wrongs that took her away from her sister so lightly. "I believe that. But that doesn't mean Jenn and I were meant to be separated. And I wonder if that was her original name or if the Drews changed her name?"

He frowned. "I never thought of it. And Jenn never said. Would people change the name of a toddler?"

"I don't know. My name was Sara and my parents changed the spelling, but kept the name. Mom said she'd always dreamed of having a little girl named Sarah, so when I arrived, I was a dream come true."

"I bet you were. I know the Drews felt the same way about Jenn, but that doesn't make it right, does it?"

"No." She tugged her coat on and looped her scarf around her neck. "I'm not blind to the joy of the situation, and these girls are a huge part of that. So maybe things do happen for a reason. Eventually." She moved toward the door and he followed her.

"Would you come with me to see the rehab center in Ellensburg tomorrow?" he asked. "We're sending the cows to auction on Monday, so if I'm going to push for this, tomorrow would be best. I'd like you with me. To offer your opinion."

"What about Kyle?"

"I'll call him. He said he was going to be tied up most of the day, but that he'd be on the ranch the rest of the weekend. Even if he's available, I want a professional opinion on things."

"Even if the profession is about a hundred degrees removed from geriatrics?"

"Let me rephrase this." He put his hands on her shoulders and looked straight at her. "I want your opinion, Sarah. If you wouldn't mind."

She wouldn't mind, but she'd be careful about pushing one way or another. She'd already done her share of that, and this decision should be Calloway, 100 percent. And given Roy's stubborn nature, she wasn't sure her advice was worth much, but she'd watched her parents deal with her grandfather's struggle. While the decisions were tough, they had to be made, and she'd hate to see this wonderful family make the wrong one.

Chapter Ten

Renzo Calloway had looked danger in the face numerous times as a county sheriff's deputy. In all these years he'd rarely quaked, but the thought of putting his father into a hated situation made his hands tremble now. Did he have the right to push for this? Was his dad up for the fight or was Renzo imposing his will on a critically ill man? Opposing arguments rattled around in his mind as he pulled into the highly acclaimed rehabilitation facility and parked the car the next morning.

Sarah rounded the hood and slung her purse over her shoulder. Then she took his hand.

She hadn't worn gloves, and the feel of her soft skin against his calloused hands seeped strength into him. She squeezed his hand lightly. "Let's see what they've got, okay? If you go in with an open mind, the confusion about choices might clear right up."

He walked through the automatic doors, her hand in his, and when they left over an hour later, he'd found his resolve after seeing videos of several patients who shared stories about their time at the rehab center. Renzo was convinced. Now the task would be convincing his mother and his stubborn and fearful father.

"There's a coffee shop about five minutes from here," he told Sarah as they walked back to the car. "I'd like a chance to talk before we get back to the girls. Coffee's on me," he added with a little bump to her shoulder.

"Cute guy buying me coffee? And time to actually relax and enjoy it? Twist my arm." She smiled up at him as he reached down to open the passenger-side door for her.

He swung the door open. She stepped by him to get into the vehicle, then paused and turned his way. She indicated the open door with a smile. "I can't tell you the last time someone opened a car door for me, Renzo, but it was probably my father and I was most likely in a booster seat."

"Then the men in Seattle are just plain stupid. And I'm okay with that." He matched her smile with his. The wind and rain had disappeared overnight, and the late November day was cold but dry. The sun shone down on her pretty hair, and the shades of gold reflected its light. "Did you know your hair shimmers in the sun?"

She didn't move to get into the car. She stayed right there, gazing up at him, and when she spoke, her voice was soft. "Does it, Renzo?"

"Oh, yeah." He reached out and gently ran his fingers over her hair. "It's beautiful, Sarah. Like you."

Her eyes searched his. He met her gaze, then dropped his eyes to her lips, not wanting to wonder anymore. He wasn't sure who leaned in first. It didn't matter.

The only thing that mattered was kissing Sarah Brown. When he was done kissing her, the first thought on his mind was wondering when he could kiss her again.

He held her close for sweet moments before letting her go. The freshly washed scent of her hair settled over him. Yes, things were fairly impossible right now, but if God granted them time, maybe they could figure this out.

"Do you know what I think?" she asked him from the curve of his arm.

"That we just shared the best kiss of all time and it put all movie kisses to shame?"

She laughed softly. "That was my first thought, of course. Mom's with the girls and it's hard to know when we can get away together, alone. Can we figure out what we'd like to do for the girls for Christmas? You can share your traditions and I can plan around them. I don't want to mess up anything that's in the works, but I do want to be part of their Christmas."

Planning Christmas with her didn't just seem right. It seemed perfect. "I think that's a great idea. And the girls' schedule in December ramps up because the pre-school does a Christmas play and the girls are supposed to be part of the angel choir."

"I can't even imagine the sweetness factor." She smiled up at him, then climbed into the car. He did the same. He drove to the coffee shop, ordered their drinks and added two slices of the shop's famous carrot cake to the order.

"Brunch," he explained when he set the cake in front

of her. "Anything with carrots in it has to be healthy, right?"

"Logical," she assured him, a big grin on her face. "Before we talk about Christmas, tell me how traumatic Monday will be. When the ridiculously big animals you all call calves go off to market."

He cringed slightly. "Chloe won't care. Naomi and Kristi might cry. The reality of raising beef hits those two harder, but it doesn't stop them from eating hamburgers and chicken. And we've always thought it was better for kids to understand where food comes from—"

"Locally sourced and farm fresh," she cut in.

"Both accurate. My mom said that Kyle and I never much worried about the outcome, but it seems little girls are different. Except our Chloe who pretends to be pragmatic in all things, but is the defendant of the underdog. Anyway, it won't be too bad. They have preschool in the morning, and the calves should be loaded before they get home. The babies start dropping in mid-January, and all three of them get wide-eyed over that."

"Do you?"

"A big, rugged cop like me?" He made a face at her and she laughed. "I suppose I do. There's something amazing about helping an animal into the world. Looking out for the calf and the mother. If the mother doesn't want to kill me," he added. He smiled at her look of surprise. "Not all cows are quiet, benevolent creatures when a cowboy messes with their newborn. Some of them take maternal instinct to a whole new level."

"I'd have never thought of that. Is it dangerous?"

"Not once you've been sideswiped by an angry

mama," he assured her. "A smart cowboy keeps a feed crib or a truck between him and possessive mothers. It's best, all around. But wrestling baby cows into the world can't hold a candle to what you do, Sarah. You save lives, every day. The tiniest of lives. I can't even imagine. Chloe and Naomi were just over four pounds when they were born. They were ridiculously small, but then Kristi was three pounds six ounces and needed an extra few weeks in the hospital to gain ground and come home. But I saw babies half the size of Chloe and Naomi and I couldn't believe it." He didn't try to hide his amazement. "How do you handle a baby that small? That fragile? I am in awe, Sarah."

She blew over her coffee to cool it before she answered. "I thought I was going to be a pediatrician like Mom. That was always the goal. But one tour of the NICU and I was hooked. It's different medicine because everything has to be miniaturized. From the meds to the equipment, to the visual aspects. Everything is so very tiny. There is nothing big and obvious and easy to treat about preemies, but the challenge called to me," she went on. "Because I saw the opportunity to make parents happy. To give them the happy ending they wanted so badly. It was as if I knew I'd be good at it. And I am," she told him but added, "but it's never about me because the NICU is a team. It's like the workings of a Swiss watch, intricate gears that keep life going, and having a whole team that knows what to do if something goes wrong. And every Christmas we decorate the NICU with cards and letters and pictures of our success stories. Those parents never forget how we all worked together to save their babies. I thank God every day that He gave me the skills to do what I do. Even if I can't cook," she finished to lighten the moment.

"Amazing."

"It is. By the way, this cake is wonderful. Is this why you brought me here? Because there are a dozen coffee shops in Ellensburg. I know. I looked because knowing how to feed my coffee habit is key."

He laughed. "They are famous for it. But it was mostly the coffee. Best blend around. So. Christmas?"

"Yes. I have to be back at work on the twenty-sixth."

"And my leave goes until January 3, so I have an extra week. I'm not sure how we'll organize things, but if Dad is back here, that would make some things easier. Here's the schedule my mom texted me now that Thanksgiving is over."

He swiped his phone and handed her the device. When she read the schedule, her eyes rounded in exaggerated surprise. "This isn't a schedule. This is a marathon."

"Agreed. I have to say I never realized how daunting this whole thing was until she sent me this text. So what you're looking at includes their school play and practices, their Christmas picture, two family holiday parties, a tree-lighting ceremony that honors veterans because my dad and his dad were both veterans, and then you throw in normal life on top of it. Oh, and breakfast with Santa, midmonth."

"What happened to the simplicity of peace on Earth, good will toward men?" she asked, then clapped her hand over her mouth. "Oh, Renzo, I'm sorry. That sounded critical, and I didn't mean it to be."

He didn't look offended. He sipped his coffee and agreed. "I think you're right. I was always working so I didn't realize how tied up the schedule got because Mom was amazing at handling it all. And she always coordinated the breakfast with Santa, but I passed that off to one of the other ladies in town who took it over happily."

"Can we simplify things?" she asked. "Shouldn't we, I mean, with all that's going on? Would that insult your mother?"

"I wish it wouldn't, but I think it would. She's trying so hard to re-create the life they might have had with their mother, and she's always afraid they'll miss something. Maybe to excess."

It did seem excessive. Nothing anyone could do would make up for the fact that the girls lost their mother before they even had a chance to know her. The busy schedule didn't allow time for the girls to just be kids. Wouldn't they lose the true meaning of Christmas in all the busyness?

"And their birthday party is scheduled for the second Saturday in December. I can't believe they're going to be four years old."

"I've never planned a kids' birthday party, and I haven't been a kid in a long time," she told him. "Who comes? Who gets invited?"

"Oh, there's a list for that, as well." He swiped past the current page to reveal a list of twenty-two names. "I don't even know who half these kids are."

Twenty-two kids? She tried to hide a cringe. "You have to invite them all? For real?"

"I guess." He stared at the list, then brought his attention back to Sarah. "We can do this. I know that. And we can't disappoint my mother, not right now, but it doesn't seem like there's a lot of time to just have fun, does it?"

"Or to be prayerful," she replied. "Or just plain grateful. Isn't Advent supposed to be a season of waiting?"

He frowned. "Of course, but there are always Christmas traditions. Aren't there?"

There were, but this schedule thrust the girls into every possible holiday trope that existed, except the ones that mattered the most. Giving of themselves.

"You hate this."

She shook her head. "I don't. I'm just surprised that there's so much in a month that's already got a lot going on."

"We can't disappoint her, Sarah."

"You're right." She wouldn't argue with him. It would be pointless and it wasn't her place, and if this is what Gina wanted for the girls, she had no right to say otherwise. And yet the agenda frustrated her. Yes, the girls were young, but they were also at an impressionable stage. Would they be able to embrace a simpler kind of holiday spirit with her? Or would they resent the changes if they eventually lived with her? And therefore resent her?

"If it gives Mom peace of mind right now, I've got to follow through on this."

He didn't say we. Funny how that shifted so quickly. She handed the phone back to him again. "Of course."

He regarded her quietly as he slipped the phone into his pocket. Gone was the sweetness of that first kiss. Gone was the camaraderie of handling things together. Clearly she wasn't allowed to inject her opinion or change the agenda to something more spiritual and even more personal for the girls.

For now.

The thought sobered her. It brought to mind her reason for being here, to gain custody of her sister's children. Not to kiss really nice detectives, or to fret over a distraught woman's infertility issues.

She'd taken time off and come east to stake a claim, and it would be foolish to lose sight of that now. There would be other Christmases, less fraught with fear and emotion. Right now, she'd do what she needed to do to keep things calm, but what she really wished was for their normal to be more like hers.

There wasn't anything she could really do about that for this year, but the girls' future?

That was a whole other thing.

He'd disappointed Sarah.

Renzo pondered that all the way back to Seattle. Kyle wasn't able to go with him. He didn't ask why. He was getting tired of his brother's excuses and negativity, so instead of asking if tomorrow would be a better day, he got into his SUV and headed west.

You're being a jerk.

He was and he knew why; because he'd seen the frustration in Sarah's eyes and he couldn't disagree with it. And yet given the situation, he wasn't about to change it, either, so there he was, stuck in the middle. While trying to make one person happy, he was disappointing another, when the whole purpose of the silly list was to make the girls happy. In the end it would most likely make them tired and fractious. Kind of like him right now.

He got to the hospital in the late afternoon. His mother and Aunt Shelly were in his father's room. His mother was fussing at his father about refusing physical therapy when Renzo walked in. Aunt Shelly looked frustrated, his mother was distraught and his father seemed stuck-in-the-mud stubborn, which wasn't unlike some cows he knew. And himself, some days.

He pulled up a chair for his mother, another for Aunt Shelly, then said his piece. "According to the doctors, we've got two choices, Dad. But based on your stubbornness and unwillingness to help yourself, we're going to be down to one choice, real quick," he told his father. "And you are absolutely going to hate it, so maybe it's time to change things up."

Roy scowled at him. He waved his better hand, but didn't try to talk although he did manage a most convincing growl.

"I know you're mad. I see it all over your face," Renzo acknowledged. "You got dealt a rough hand, and I'm sorry about that. We all are. We'd change it if we could, but we can't. If you're willing to throw in the towel and say 'This is it,' then so be it. That's your choice," Renzo stressed, and he had to ignore the way his heart tugged when he read the hopelessness in his father's eyes. "But you have already defied really high odds by making it this far. They've done some pretty impressive repairs to your heart and brain, but if you don't do your part, then your worst fear is about to be realized and you'll end up in a skilled nursing facility, waiting to die."

"Lorenzo." His mother's sharp intake of breath italicized his name, but Aunt Shelly gave him a silent thumbs-up behind his mother's back.

"I'm not going to sugarcoat this, Mom. We can't," he told her. "We're running out of time. Dad, if you don't start cooperating, you're going to lose even more function and eventually there is no way back. But if you start listening—"

His father glowered and did his best to fold his arms, even though the left side didn't want to cooperate.

"—and trying, you can begin retraining your brain and your muscles to react again. Is it going to be hard? Yes. Tiring? Absolutely. Successful?" Renzo paused and held his father's gaze. "I don't know. But if you refuse to try, then we have no other choice and they'll release you to a nursing home without rehabilitation options because why waste the room on someone who is refusing rehabilitation?"

"Can't move." His father groaned the words from an uncooperative mouth, but Renzo didn't cave. He couldn't afford to cave.

"With time and effort you could. The man I know, the man who raised me to stand strong no matter what the odds, to face each day with my feet firmly on the ground, always said he wanted to die in the saddle. With his boots on. So now it's up to you. I can't tell you it won't be a tough road back, but you've never shied away from a rough road before, Dad. I can't imagine why you'd want to do it now with so much waiting for you at home. So much to live for."

His mother had been staring at him, as if unnerved by his audacity, but when she turned back to Roy, she crossed her arms and followed Lorenzo's lead. "He's right, Roy. And you know it. And it's not about having a farm to run and work to do, because there's always plenty of that to go around and maybe you'd like a break from all that, anyway. It's about being part of our boys' lives. Raising the girls. Being with family and friends, and if the good Lord was calling you home, my guess is you'd already be there. You're not, and Renzo's right. Maybe it's time to realize that God saved you for a reason. Not that sweet young doctor or Renzo or the paramedics, but God, Himself. And if that doesn't give you the gumption to pick up the fight, I don't know what will."

She stopped talking.

Renzo stayed quiet, too. He stood at the end of the bed, praying he wasn't being an insensitive jerk, but when his father turned his head away, and a tear slipped down Roy's weathered, weakened cheek, Renzo's heart slipped with it.

"Go."

His father wanted him to leave. That only exacerbated the pain in Renzo's chest. He turned to leave. His mother reached out for him, but what could she say?

He'd taken a shot and missed the target. That wasn't something that happened in his job, and yet it seemed to be happening with remarkable frequency in his life.

"I'll call you later," she whispered. "And Renzo, thank you." She gripped his sleeve tightly. "Thank you for your honesty, for taking a stand."

For all the good it did.

He walked out, not wanting to upset his father further. Maybe the fight looked too hard, or the climb too high. Only his dad could make that decision.

He got to the elevator just as Aunt Shelly reached his side. "You did good, kid," she told him. "Buy me coffee, and we'll let them stew on your words. You don't mind buying an old lady a cup of coffee, do you?"

"I don't know any old ladies," he told her, and loved seeing her smile. "But I'd be honored to buy my beautiful aunt a cup of joe. I hear they've got one of those famous coffeehouses nearby."

"Well, it *is* Seattle," she teased back. "And I could go for an extra-hot macchiato right about now while I thank you for saying what I've been wanting to say the past week. If my Charlie were here, he'd be fighting tooth and nail to spend another week with me. To gain a little more time with the kids and the grandkids. To see Roy give up like that made me angry. But you've said what needed to be said, and now we'll give it time to sink in."

"I don't want him to hate me."

Shelly gripped his arm snugly. "There's no chance of that. He raised you to be forthright and honest, and that's what I saw in there. Now the choice is up to him. We'll just pray him to the right one, eh?"

"Yes." They found a coffee shop downstairs. He bought her coffee and they sat in a windowed waiting room, drinking it. They didn't talk about Roy and his choices.

They talked about her kids and grandkids and what they were doing for Christmas. And of course, how much they would miss their father during the holiday season. And when tears slipped down Aunt Shelly's cheeks, he tugged her into a big hug. If Roy Calloway was his usual self, he'd understand the ramifications of his choices. How those choices would hurt his wife and his sons and those precious girls. But he wasn't himself, and Renzo drove home, half-wishing he hadn't taken a stand and knowing he had no other choice. He wanted to talk with Sarah. Tell her what he'd done, but Sarah wasn't waiting in the house like he expected. Kyle was. And he shrugged into his coat before Renzo even got up the back steps.

"Where's Sarah?"

"Went home. She needed to do some things and asked if I'd step in. She said her mom was spending the weekend back in Seattle with her father."

She was putting some space between them. Space he didn't want, but probably deserved because his options were narrowed by circumstances out of his control. "Thanks, Kyle."

His brother shrugged. "How was Dad? Same as yesterday?"

Renzo nodded as he slung his jacket on a hook inside the door. "Yeah. I yelled at him."

Kyle had been about to turn toward the front door. He stopped. "You did?"

"Kind of. Yes."

"Man, you're something, Renzo."

A flash of anger thrummed along Renzo's spine. Something? He'd give him "something."

"I wanted to do that yesterday," Kyle admitted, and his words made the flash of anger disappear. "I wanted to tell him to at least try. Try to do the therapy, try to follow directions, try to regain control of his body because our father never gives up on anything. He never has, so seeing him like that, feeling sorry for himself, stabbed me in the gut. How am I supposed to be strong if my father falls apart?"

"You've always got me, Kyle. We're brothers. I'd never turn my back on you. And if there's ever anything I can do to help you with whatever's going on, I'm here for you."

Kyle choked back a sigh. "I wish it was that easy," he replied. "But it's not. Probably never is. Gotta go." He pulled the door open and started to step outside, then turned back. "Thanks, Renzo. I know I'm not on top of my game, and I don't know when I will be. But I appreciate the backup. More than you know."

"We've got this," Renzo assured him, but when Kyle shut the door, Renzo sighed.

They didn't have it. Not really. Not yet, anyway, but if they stuck together, they could make a difference to the ranch at least.

He trudged back into the kitchen. There, on the wall, above a couple of cute pictures of the girls was one of his grandmother's wall hangings. She'd done all kinds of needlework in her day, but this one was her favorite and his mother had hung it in the kitchen as a daily reminder. *Thy Will Be Done*...

That was it. Short. Straightforward. Succinct.

A biblical direction to put everything into God's hands. Renzo stared at the simple prayer.

He didn't like handing over control of anything. Not his life, his work, his family. The detective in him was often questioning circumstances, timing and sometimes God. Why would Jenn die and leave three premature infants? Why would a just God take her?

"Renzo?"

A plaintive voice called to him from upstairs. He moved to the stairway and looked up. "What's up, honey?"

A sad face looked back at him. "I wet the bed."

Naomi. She'd had a recurring problem with bedwetting that they thought they fixed with a buzzer system that helped wake her, but Kyle wouldn't have known about that. He never requested details about the girls, or their problems. "No worries. We've got this." He went upstairs, changed her bedding and when she'd climbed into warm, dry pajamas, he tucked her back into bed. He went to kiss her good-night, but her silent tears surprised him. "Hey. What's up? This isn't a big deal, honey. It happens to everyone now and again."

"But I'll have different jammies on," she whispered, the catch in her voice ramping up his sympathy.

Of course it was always on "high" when it concerned these girls. They owned him, completely, and he was okay with that. "Then everyone will know I wet the bed again."

"By everyone, you mean your sisters," he said softly. "Because you already know I don't care. And why would you be afraid to have Chloe and Kristi know you had an accident? Isn't that what family is for? To love one another? To stand by each other?"

"They'll think I'm a baby," she whispered. "I don't want anybody to think I'm a baby. I just want this to stop happening."

Truthfully, he hadn't given much thought to her buzzer system in the past few weeks, so he couldn't fault Kyle for this one. "We'll use the buzzer every night again, just long enough for your body to remember to wake up. Okay?"

She frowned, and a tiny shuddering sob wrenched hold of his heart, but then she nodded. "'Kay. I'm sorry I forgot."

"Oh, sweet thing." He reached down and hugged her. "Me, too. Silly us. Now we'll remember. And when your jammies are clean, I'll bring them up to you, all right?"

Relief eased her delicate features. "Okay. Thank you, Renzo. Love you." She yawned.

"Love you, too." He tiptoed out, put everything into the washing machine and started it.

There were several single parents on the force. A few guys and two women. He used to shrug off their dilemmas as poor planning.

What an idiot he'd been, because life resisted planning when it revolved around kids, cars and electricity. A problem with any one of the three could throw a single parent's life into a temporary tailspin. Till now, he'd never sympathized with it because there'd been three of them raising the girls. As a party of one, he realized his limitations.

And if Sarah took custody of the girls, how would she handle all of this? The thought of a live-in nanny raising the girls hit him square in the chest. He didn't want a stranger having that kind of influence on them. No stranger could know them like the Calloways did. And yet if Jenn had known about Sarah, the girls would probably have been left in her care. There was absolutely no reason they shouldn't be in her care, except that Jenn hadn't known and the Calloways had stepped in for four wonderful years. The thought of stepping away was wrong. So wrong. But so was what happened to Sarah and Jenn.

He turned on a college football game while he waited for the laundry to be done, and when he'd gently changed a very sleepy Naomi back into her original pajamas, he finally went to bed.

Sleep was a long time coming that night, and when it finally did, images of his father and the girls floated around in his dreams. For the first time in his adult life, he woke up unsure of what he should do.

And that didn't work for Renzo Calloway. Not by a long shot.

Chapter Eleven

Sarah approached the front desk of the nursing home with a confidence she didn't feel, and when a young woman brought Lanny Drew to the visiting room, nerves sent a shiver up her spine. The aide set the brakes on the wheelchair, made sure Lanny was comfortable, then walked away to the desk in the nearby reception area.

Sarah took a deep breath. "Thank you for seeing me, Mr. Drew."

"Call me Lanny. Please," he added, sighing as she took a seat across from him. "I don't mean to stare at you. It's only because you look so much like her, you know? I see you and I think of Jenn and how much she meant to us. Then my girl was gone and the triplets were born and I couldn't take care of them. It felt like everything was over even though their lives were just beginning. With other people," he added. "And that felt wrong, too, but there were no other choices. I couldn't have taken on caring for three babies even if I were healthy, which I wasn't, but it sure felt like everything that had been normal became abnormal in just a few months' time."

"It had to be so difficult for you. And I'm so very sorry for your loss, Lanny."

"You'd have liked her," he said gruffly. "I didn't like her decision to go ahead and have a baby, but Jenn was one to go her own way most times. Still, the thought of those three girls has kept me going this long. In my own way, I'm happy for that. They got to know me some and I'm glad. They're amazing, aren't they?"

"They are," she agreed. "I find myself marveling at them. So much alike, yet so different."

"Something that makes no sense," he told her. "Considering they're identical."

"Renzo reminded me that their genetics might be the same, but their souls are their own."

Lanny surprised her with a snort. "I used to hang on to all that. When my wife passed away, at least I had Jenn. I centered everything around her. Then suddenly things went bad when she was expecting the girls and I think of how many times I prayed for my wife, then for Jenn, and it got me nothing. Absolutely nothing. It's easier to shrug it all off now. Way easier than trying to figure out how a loving God allows so much sadness in the world."

"It's hard to be optimistic when you're sick," she sympathized. "When your body fails you. Or when you're in pain."

He drew his brows down and in. "And when your whole world is taken from you. That, too."

And yet there were the girls, three amazing blessings. The Lord giveth and He taketh away. But she wasn't here to argue about faith with this man. He was hurting emotionally and physically and maybe seeing her made things worse. She leaned slightly closer to him. "Can you tell me about Jenn? Would you mind?"

"I wouldn't mind." He contemplated her for a moment. "She was lovely, like you. And she had a good head on her shoulders. I think she was like her mama that way."

His words didn't just startle Sarah. They shocked her. "I don't understand. How would you know that?"

"The letter." His expression indicated surprise. "The one that came with her when we picked her up in Seattle. We saved it for her, of course. No names on it, nothing to indicate who she was, that's how she wanted it, but the letter was real nice and showed the kind of person she was."

Sarah didn't expect the surge of raw emotion, so when it blindsided her, she wasn't prepared. "Jenn got a letter?"

Tears obstructed her vision and when she tried to dash them away, more took their place.

"You didn't?"

It was hard to form words around the solid lump in her throat. She swiped at her eyes with a tissue and shook her head. "No. I did not."

"I'm sorry." The old fellow became distraught. "I didn't mean to make you sad. I just thought if Jenn had a letter, you had one, too."

A letter from her mother. Did it explain her choices?

Why she gave away two beautiful daughters? Why she closed the door firmly on any future relationship?

Sarah grabbed another tissue from the nearby table and composed herself as best she could. The last thing she wanted to do was upset this sick man. "I'll check with my parents, but I'm pretty sure if there was a letter, they'd have shared it with me. What did it say? Do you still have it?"

"It said she was sorry. Real sorry, but that she was doing what was best all around. I don't rightly know where the letter is. When they moved me in here, things got muddled. And Jenn had the letter, last I knew, so it might be somewhere packed up with her things. Renzo might know. Or Gina, more likely."

Gina, who was caught in her own desperate situation right now, fighting for the life of her husband.

You've waited this long. You've had a great life. Take a breath and remember why you're here.

She took the mental advice and Lanny's hand. "I'll check on it. And sorry I got emotional," she told him softly. "But it's all such emotional stuff, isn't it?"

"It is," he replied. "I've shed my share of tears, but Jenn was a strong one. She did so well in school and beyond, and she was respected by everyone that worked with her up in Wenatchee. Her patients loved her, and she stood by them. She never cared if they were rich or poor. She took everyone as a child of God. And when I'd get mad at God, she'd hug me and say 'Daddy, you've got to get hold of yourself because one of these days you're going to run out of time to tell God you're sorry.

We've been blessed by so much. Let's just cling to that, okay?'"

"She sounds wonderful."

"Well, she was, and that's why I get so mad when I think about why she died so young. It makes no sense, not a lick of sense, and when folks told me that my Mary was probably up there, with her arms out, waiting for our girl, I near got sick to my stomach because I didn't want them up there. I wanted them here. With me. And if that's the way God does business, I wanted no part of it. Not then. Not now."

His grief made her chest ache. He hadn't gotten over the anger of one loss before he'd faced another one, and now he was just plain mad. Especially at God. She changed the subject purposely. "Did Jenn have boyfriends?"

That made him laugh. "Yes. And no. She had a bunch, then kind of shrugged them off as she built her career. Maybe there wasn't the right one, maybe she set her standards too high. For whatever reason, she dated here and there but said there wasn't anyone truly special. There were a couple I thought might work, but they faded away, if you know what I mean."

His words almost exactly described her romantic history—until she met Renzo Calloway a few weeks ago. There was no denying the spark there. And their kiss had ignited more than a spark. How she wished the timing was different. "I know exactly what you mean," she told him, referencing the romances that faded with time. "Is that when she decided to become a single mother?"

"Against my wishes, but yes. She examined her options all the time, but she felt like time might be running out because she was in her thirties and no likely prospects loomed on the horizon. So she jumped in with both feet, like she always did, then tragedy hit."

"But we've got the girls."

His lips thinned. His voice dropped. "I already had my girl, you see? And as much as I love those little ones, it's not the same because I won't be here to be part of their lives the way I was with my Jennifer. I carried her in my arms. I taught her how to ride a bike. I coached her softball team, drove her to saxophone lessons and dance recitals and stood in the pouring rain to watch her in the marching band. Watched her graduate from high school and the university. She was my heart. When she got taken away, and the girls were so little, there was nothing I could do to help." He indicated his fading body with a sorrowed glance. "I had some money, money I could have left them, but being here in the home will sap all of that, too. So in the end, I have nothing to give those three little girls that they can't get from someone else, because I will never be there for them the way I was there for Jenn. And that's the sum of it. So maybe you finding us when you did is a good thing, because you're more a part of Jenn than anyone else in the picture. And there's something to be said for that, much as I love the Calloways. You're her blood, and that still means something."

He probably meant the words to hearten her.

They tore at her instead. Yes, she was the girls' biological aunt, but they'd bonded with the Calloways, and

she couldn't simply dismiss that fact. But while she recognized the goodness of the Calloway family, they were
being torn by a variety of factors right now. Was it right
to have the girls be in the middle of all that? What was
in their best interests?

Lanny yawned.

That was her cue to let the ailing man rest. She stood
up, leaned down and gently hugged him. "Thank you
for talking with me. For telling me about my sister. It
means a lot to me, Lanny."

"She'd have loved you if she had the chance," he
told her. Then he gripped her hand with unexpected
strength. "We would have, too. And it's disheartening
to think that none of us knew what they did way back
then because we wouldn't have allowed it, and I expect
your parents feel the same way."

"They do."

"Can you tell Renzo to keep the girls home today? I
don't think I'm up for a visit from them."

She'd sapped his energy, and now he wouldn't be
able to enjoy his granddaughters. The realization made
her feel selfish.

His hand went lax as he yawned again. The aide
crossed the floor. "I can help you back to your room,
Mr. Drew."

He didn't speak. Weariness seemed to wash over
him, and when the aide began moving down the hall,
the elderly man's chin dropped to his chest.

Her visit had worn him out. Yes, she'd wanted to
hear about her sister, but not at the girls' expense. She
drove back to the Calloway ranch. Kyle and a borrowed

hand were moving cattle into a lower pen, closer to the graveled driveway. The days of Advent would begin tomorrow, a sweet time of anticipation. The young cows would be gone on Monday. She still had a few weeks to be here, to be part of the Christmas preparation and while her ideas were different from Gina's, she wanted this to be a beautiful holiday season for her three nieces. Maybe her presence would offer some calm to their overburdened schedule. If nothing else, she'd be here to celebrate their fourth birthday with them. That alone was a reason to celebrate.

Sarah had been right about the girls' December calendar and Renzo was kicking himself for not realizing it sooner. He was studying the overbooked schedule when she came in the side door late Saturday morning. She slung her cute jacket on a hook, laid her scarf on it and came his way. She looked troubled and that only compounded his guilt. "I made you feel bad yesterday, and I'm sorry about that. You've got enough on your plate without a stranger coming along and criticizing what you've got planned for Christmas, especially since your family has done such a marvelous job raising the girls. I want to apologize, Renzo." She slipped into one of the seats flanking the broad end of the island. "I'm more than happy to jump in and help in whatever way I can, and I'll do it nicely."

"You weren't wrong." He slid the December calendar her way. "You were right, and the reason I got mad was because I don't want to disappoint my mother or worry her when she's already so worried, but it was a knee-jerk reaction, Sarah, and I apologize. Truce?" He raised a hand to high-five her.

"Yes. Please."

She raised her hand, too, but he didn't give her a high five. He took her hand in his and surprised her by kissing it instead. She frowned at him. "Hey."

He didn't let go quickly. He took the time to smile into her eyes, then paused just long enough for her to smile back. Then he lightly squeezed her hand and released it before indicating the calendar. "The birthday party stays. Everything else is up for discussion."

"Really?"

"Hey, I'm flexible. Eventually. Tell me what you think."

"The school play should stay. They're already committed to it, and I think being in an angel choir is absolutely wonderful. And I saw that the town does a Candlelighting Walk next Saturday, where they light the candles in all the churches in the village, then decorate the outdoor crèche with evergreen branches. That's more in keeping with the spirit of Christmas than breakfast with Santa, isn't it?"

"I think that's a great idea. And we can always take the girls to see Santa at the mall."

"And we could do that on a weekday because these four weekends are so busy."

"Everyone will understand if we bow out of a family party," he continued. "They all know how sick Dad is, and no one on the Calloway side will care. The Altobellis will give us a measure of guilt because they love seeing the girls, but they'll understand, too. So let's delete those from the schedule, too."

"Are you sure they won't be offended?"

He shrugged. "They don't like it when folks flout tradition, but in the end they would want us to do what's best for the girls. They know we're dealing with a lot. And we'll see Mom's family for Christmas Eve services. We always go to that particular service. That's the more important thing, right?"

"Yes." A tiny frown formed a wrinkle between her brows. "You know you didn't have to do this. I shouldn't have said anything. I didn't mean to mess up your mother's plans, and I should have been more sensitive to that. The sheer number of activities and events took me by surprise, that's all."

"Same here," he replied. "And I shouldn't have let my protective instincts jump into high gear, but they seem to be ultrasensitized with everything that's going on with Dad. I honestly didn't have a true understanding of how busy the month of December was because Mom handled most of it on her own the past few years, but you made a good point. How can anyone relax and enjoy the season if they're running around keeping commitments every day?"

"They can't."

"Exactly. So let's get rid of this Christmas picture thing, too. Would you be willing to take a Christmas-themed photo of the girls this week? That way it's natural and I can send them out to family as Christmas cards."

"I'd love it. We could do it today, actually, because I

went to see Lanny this morning and tired him out. That wasn't my intention."

She hadn't mentioned that she was going to do that. He waited for her to say more.

"He asked me to have you keep the girls home today, so that's another thing I need to apologize for. Taking their time with their grandpa away from them."

"You didn't tire him," said Renzo. "The disease did. We can take the girls to see him on Monday. By the time we're home from church tomorrow, he's likely to be worn out. Mornings are best for him right now. Did you ask him about Jenn? And are you ready for coffee? Because I am." He stood up and made a beeline for the coffee maker.

"I am always ready for coffee, and yes, we talked about Jenn. I wanted to see her from his perspective. I know you were her close friend, but he was her father. I wanted to hear what he thought, what she was like and what she did through his eyes."

"And he told you."

"It was so sweet. And sad." She didn't cry, but he read the sympathy in her expression. "He's so angry at God."

"Lanny's been angry at God for a long time."

"So he said. I wish he wasn't. I wish he could be at peace with everything that happened. But then I'm not totally at peace with it, either, so there's that."

"Lanny's a good man, but he's never been what you would call an optimist. And he didn't like Jenn's idea of having a baby on her own, but Jenn did things her way. When it all went bad, I think his grief was magnified by his guilt that he'd spent the last months of her life scolding her for her decision. And when we found out about the triplets early on, he immediately looked up every reason why multiple births were more dangerous and shared them with her."

"Oh no."

He made a face of consternation as he brewed the coffee. "Yeah. It wasn't pretty. But Jenn just hugged him and said she was aware of the possibilities, although she was incredibly surprised by the turn of events. She was always hugging him. Reassuring him. Teasing him. She wanted him to come back to a full life. Full faith. To get over his anger, and losing her only magnified the situation. Grief is a powerful thing."

"I've watched it tear families apart and pull some together, but it's a wretched bend in the road," she told him as she accepted the cup of coffee. "When I chose my specialty, my mom told me that it wasn't the level of constant detail that messed with neonatologists. It was the roller-coaster ride of wins and losses that tore folks apart, so we hold the wins close and pray through the losses. And our team works through things together. That's a huge part of our success."

"It's the same on the force," he told her. "The things we see on the job show us both sides of human nature, the good and the bad. We've got a great bunch of men and women, and that helps a lot."

She sipped her coffee and smiled her thanks. "Perfect."

Her reaction made him smile, too. "Well, it was a lot of work, tucking that pod into the system and pressing a button."

A noise from above shifted his attention. "The on-slaught begins. I told them we'd do the gingerbread house once you were here. I thawed some frosting Mom had in the freezer and put it in one of these bags she uses. Easy-peasy, right?" He indicated quick step-by-step instructions on the box of premade walls.

"So it would seem."

Thirty minutes and three disgruntled girls later he was ready to replace the bag of frosting with actual cement. "This is impossible," he muttered when a second wall tipped over. "They make it look so easy on TV."

"Outtakes," Sarah whispered. "How do we get the walls to stand up while the frosting dries?" Sarah whis-pered in desperation.

"I don't know," he whispered back. "Because it doesn't really dry. Not all the way."

Chloe tapped a pack of the squishy snowmen and frowned. "How can these guys protect the house if we can't even build the house?" She posed the question with her distinctive eye roll.

Sarah hit a button on her phone. Renzo heard only her half of the conversation, but when she hung up, she did a quick internet search for something. Then she pointed to the page that popped up and said, "Mom says this is what we need. Royal frosting. It dries like cement."

"That sounds awful. Is it still edible?" he asked, and she nodded.

"Totally. Just really, really hard-drying." She fol-lowed the recipe while Naomi and Kristi carefully opened bags of candy decorations.

Chloe propped an elbow on the island counter and put her chin in her hand. "I bet Mama Gina knows about this stuff." She aimed a dubious look toward Sarah and the mixer. "She knows lots of stuff."

"She sure does," noted Renzo. "Like how to be kind and make people feel good about things. A lesson I believe she's shared with all three of you, correct?" he asked with a pointed look in her direction. "And I'm pretty sure my mother has never made a gingerbread house," he added, "so you might be sadly mistaken. Be nice. Please."

"I love being nice!" Naomi assured them as she poured nonpareils into a small bowl. "God wants us to be nice, so why not be nice all the time. Right?"

"That's silly if you don't even feel like being nice, Naomi." Chloe started to make a face, but then redirected her attention to Sarah before Renzo could scold her again. "'Cept it *is* really nice to make these, I think. If it works," she added grudgingly, and he couldn't fault her for that because the outcome wasn't looking very good at the moment.

"My mom used to make these with me when I was a kid," Sarah explained to Chloe. "She called it making memories because she didn't really like gingerbread. She just wanted to do something fun with me. Once we get the walls and roof constructed, I'll take pictures while you girls decorate the house, okay? We'll send those to Mama Gina and Papa."

"And that will make her smile." Chloe sat up straighter. "I think it's hard to smile when people are in the hospital."

"It's hard to smile when you're sad or worried," Sarah agreed.

"But maybe Nomi's right. Maybe we should try harder. So nobody worries?"

"Yes." Sarah met Chloe's gaze, and the love in her eyes fist-clenched Renzo's heart. "We should always try, darling."

He slipped away to get a new frosting bag, but not before the image imprinted on his mind. Sarah and the three girls, creating memories together. The moment brought reality into focus.

They belong together.

The realization broadsided him. If Jenn had been given the chance to know her younger sister, she would have left the girls in Sarah's care.

He saw it plainly, but how was he going to broach the subject with his mother?

He had no idea. His father's condition cast a pall on everything, but he'd have to talk to her at some point. He'd suddenly realized that if this whole mess came down to a court case, he'd have to take Sarah's side. Not because she was better for the kids. He was proud enough of his family to know their worth. And not because he had feelings for her.

But because if Jenn had been aware of this wonderful woman, she'd have chosen her as guardian for her daughters. And that made all the difference. But how could he make this better in the meantime?

He'd start with adjusting the girls' schedule, he decided when the girls were decorating the gingerbread house two hours later. The walls were finally staying upright and the roof was solidly set in place.

The girls loved diving into creative things like this. They'd have more time for that if he lightened things up. He'd let his mom know about the changes, certain she'd understand.

He drove to Seattle after church the following morning. The girls had insisted he bring the gingerbread house and the pictures Sarah had taken. He strode into the hospital, convinced he was right.

Unfortunately, his mother didn't see it the same way.

She didn't just object to the girls missing parties and events. She insisted that they follow the schedule she'd given him to the letter. It wasn't a suggestion, either. It was more like a direct order, so if he did make the changes, he'd be adding another layer of anxiety to her already full plate.

On the flip side, if he didn't loosen things up for the girls, his conscience would suffer.

In the end, his conscience won. He was there with the girls. His mom wasn't. He'd do what he thought best and they'd argue about it later, because prioritizing the children's joy was his goal. They'd been handed a difficult scenario a few weeks ago. He wasn't about to do anything to make that any worse.

Chapter Twelve

Sarah saw Gina Calloway's number pop up on her phone and took the call the day before the girls' Christmas play the following week. "Hi, Mrs. Calloway. How are you?"

"Call me Gina, please," Renzo's mother replied. "I feel that since we both care for so many of the same people, Mr. and Mrs. is far too formal. Don't you agree, Sarah?"

Care for so many of the same people?

She meant the girls, of course, because there was no way Gina Calloway could know of Sarah's growing feelings for her son. "Agreed. How is Mr. Cal—" She caught herself before she finished. "How is Roy doing?"

"Stubborn. Always was. Still is. I'm hoping he'll see the error of his ways," Gina said roundly.

The way she said it clued Sarah in. "He can hear you, can't he?"

"Yes."

Gina was trying to goad her husband toward recovery. It wasn't a trick Sarah could use on preemies, but she'd seen colleagues use it on older patients with a measure of success. "I'm hoping he listens."

"You can lead a horse to water…"

Gina didn't finish the adage. She didn't have to. "I hear you. Did you like the girls' Christmas pics? And the gingerbread house project?" Renzo had taken the gingerbread house and candid photos of the girls to Seattle on his last two visits.

"We loved them," gushed Gina. "They looked beautiful. I could tell instantly who was who and you can't always do that with them."

You sure couldn't. Sarah was still watching for the tiny mole on Kristi's neck and the way Naomi thrust up her left brow. The right brow was Chloe. "I'm glad you liked them. And I didn't know what a ham Kristi was until I took out the camera."

"She's always loved being noticed," Gina explained. "She'd peep little noises in the NICU to get people to make eye contact with her. And I know they say they can't smile that young, but she definitely did, so what do they know? She loved having folks pay attention to her. She was her own little person, right from the very beginning. Now, Sarah, Renzo gave me the revised schedule for the girls when he came to visit last week."

Here it was. The reckoning she'd expected when Renzo said their new schedule hadn't exactly been well received. Sarah took a deep breath. "Yes."

"It's not right, dear." Gina's voice wasn't mean, but it wasn't anything to mess with, either. "I tried to talk to my son, but he was adamant, so I'm calling you. To change up the girls' holiday customs messes with their continuity. Just because I can't be there to take care of things doesn't give anyone carte blanche to rearrange their lives. And to change our traditions while Roy is sick and I'm in Seattle seems wrong. As if you're taking advantage of the situation."

Taking advantage?

Her?

Sarah bit back her initial response because she'd purposely avoided using Roy's illness to gain an advantage.

"I know you and your mother have been a tremendous help to Renzo with the girls, but they've already had so much disruption to their lives. I want their holidays to be as picture-perfect as I can make them, even in my absence. I made sure my son understood that, but I wanted to share my feelings with you, too. The girls have gone through enough, don't you think?"

The girls didn't seem to remember a lot of detail about their previous Christmases, other than a few endearing television specials, the beautiful crèche they'd put on a broad sideboard in the dining room and the much larger outside Nativity scene. And all three recalled sugar cookies and twinkle lights. There didn't seem to be any real boundaries when it came to the triplets and twinkle lights.

Other than that, they seemed happy to do just about anything, but Sarah wasn't about to argue with their legal guardian. And yet she couldn't live with herself and not stand her ground. "You've done such a wonderful job with the girls that they're quite resilient, actually. I'm leaving the scheduling in Renzo's very capable hands. He's got a knack for working with them. They love him."

"They love all of us." Gina wasn't being obtuse. She sounded matter-of-fact. "And now that they know they have an aunt, I fear we're setting them up for disappointment. The fact that you look so much like their mother could confuse them, and that's a genuine concern. And I have all the concerns I can handle right now."

"You do," Sarah answered. She took a deep breath because she longed to argue her point, but didn't. "We'll iron out details once Roy is better. I'm sure we all want what's best for the girls. You focus on him. We've got this."

"You've got this for a few more weeks." There was no missing the pointed note in Gina's tone. "And then you'll be back to work, Renzo will be back to work and we'll have Roy closer, one way or another. Either way, I'll be back with my girls."

My girls.

The deliberate phrase made Sarah suck in a breath.

"Thanks for pitching in, Sarah. You've been a big help to Renzo and Kyle."

Kyle.

Did Gina have any idea what Kyle and Valerie were going through? Valerie had pleaded for privacy. Did that mean the entire family was unaware of the frustrations the couple faced daily? Still, it wasn't her place to say anything. Their family. Their rules. "I'm glad. And please know that I'm praying for Roy's complete recovery."

"As are we. But we need to get beyond his boneheadedness first, it seems. I appreciate your understanding, Sarah. Goodbye."

Sarah cringed once she disconnected the call.

Gina was a strong woman who'd had two major things yanked out of her control. Her husband's life was hanging by a precarious thread, and the children she'd planned on adopting had a new family member show up out of the blue at the worst possible time.

The phone call was proof positive that Renzo's mother viewed Sarah as a threat.

Sarah would prefer being thought of as an asset, but she *was* threatening the status quo. She'd come here to do exactly that. Was asking to keep the children's holiday more faith-centered a bad thing?

No. But if she pushed and it became a grown-up squabble, the girls might resent her interference. On the other hand, if the judge overseeing the plea for adoption remained unaware of Roy's health crisis, he or she could make a ruling any day without knowing of Sarah's existence or the current conditions affecting the Calloway family.

Sarah reached for the phone.

She didn't want to do this. Every fiber of her being protested against it, but she was wise enough to know that once the adoption had been approved, having her say in court would be much harder. Quietly, and somewhat sadly, she gave her lawyer the go-ahead to inform the court of the current conditions, then drove to the Calloways' ranch. She'd tell Renzo what she'd done. He'd either understand or he wouldn't. No way did she want him blindsided by any of this, but when she got to the house, he met her at the door with a bundled-up child. Kristi, she realized, when she spotted the tiny mole.

"Fever of 104 and it's not going down with medication. The doctor wants to see her. Can you take Chloe and Naomi to school? It's their last play practice before the big day."

"Of course. Oh, sweet baby." She pressed a quick and gentle kiss to Kristi's dry, hot skin. "Auntie is praying for you. Go." She stepped aside so that Renzo could get through the door. "I've got this."

"Is Kristi okay?" Naomi and Chloe were standing side by side in the kitchen. Hands clutched, they stared at Renzo's departing back. Worry drew mirror image lines in the girls' faces.

Sarah hugged them both before she peeled off her jacket. "Kids get sick all the time, don't they?"

Naomi nodded, but Chloe folded her arms. "I don't think that's, like, a real answer. Do you?"

She'd called her out for hedging the question, just like Renzo had done her first day in town. "You're right. It's not, and that's because I don't have a real answer right now," Sarah replied. "We know she's sick. We know the doctors can help. But that's all we know. Except, what cheers people up when they're sick?"

"Cookies!" Chloe looked quite sure of herself.

"And freeze pops!" added Naomi.

"Oh. Fizzy pop, too," Chloe added. "Like when your tummy is weird, Mama Gina always gives me fizzy pop," she said firmly.

Not to be outdone, Naomi chimed in, "Fizzy pop with ice cream that gets all creamy and bubbly."

"You two are wonderful," she told them as she pretended to weigh their contributions. "We've got freeze pops in the freezer, and we can't make fizzy sodas with Kristi gone, so what does that leave us?"

"Cookies!" Naomi fist-pumped the air. "She will love cookies so much, won't she? When she's better."

And it would help keep these two occupied while Renzo tended to their sister. "What kind?"

"Chocolate chip is her most favorite."

"Mine, too," added Chloe. "All three of us like them a lot."

"Well, who doesn't?" Sarah teased. "And we've got my mom's recipe taped inside this cupboard. I'm actually getting somewhat comfortable in the kitchen, girls. Let's do this." They spent the next few hours making cookies, then she took the girls to their afternoon preschool class. The teacher met her at the door.

"We're short one angel, it seems."

"Kristi's sick," Sarah told her as the other girls hooked their jackets and hats in the cubby corner. "The angel choir will probably have to go on without her tomorrow."

"I'm so sorry." The young teacher frowned. "She was so looking forward to this. She loves being in front of an audience."

"We'll sing extra loud, Miss Mamie." Naomi came closer to reassure her teacher. "I promise."

"Oh, Naomi, thank you." The teacher palmed Naomi's cheek, then winked at Sarah once Naomi and Chloe had moved to the gathering table. "Extra loud is just what we need," she whispered to Sarah in jest.

"I'm sure it is. I'm going shopping for their birthday party," she told the teacher. "My mother will pick the girls up today, all right?"

"Fine." The teacher stepped into the classroom and closed the door.

Sarah hurried to the adjacent parking area. She texted her mother about picking the girls up, then hurried to Quincy to buy party supplies for the weekend birthday bash. When her phone buzzed nearly three hours later, the message took her by complete surprise. No one has come for the girls. ETA?

Sarah was in the middle of checking out from the third store. She texted back quickly. I'm so sorry! In Quincy, can be there in twenty minutes. I don't know what happened.

It took long, drawn seconds for the teacher to text her back, and Sarah sensed her frustration in the message. Doctor's appointment for my daughter in twenty minutes. Must change it.

Guilt hit Sarah. She called her mother right away. "Mom, where are you? You were supposed to pick up the girls this afternoon while I was shopping for birthday stuff. Did you get my text about Kristi?"

"Sarah, no. I didn't receive a text. Oh, darling, I'm sorry, but I'm only five minutes from the school," Lindsay replied. "I'll get them right now and meet you back at the house. I was out Christmas shopping and no texts came in. I am so sorry."

"No, my bad. I should have called and spoken to you directly. I know better than to rely on texting when something is really important," Sarah replied. "It's just so easy. Yes, go get them if you can. I'll call the teacher and let her know. It's just two of them. Kristi's sick and had to go to the doctor. I'll see you in half an hour."

"Perfect."

Her heart calmed by the time she got back to the house. Renzo's SUV was there. That meant Kristi was back home. Her mother's car was tucked alongside, so the girls had been picked up from school. She parked her car, grabbed two armloads of shopping bags and headed up the steps.

Renzo was waiting just inside the door. The girls were nowhere to be seen, and her mother was off to the side. To say that Lindsay Brown didn't look happy was the understatement of the century.

Sarah hurried through the door. "What's wrong?" She loosened her fingers from the assortment of bags and let them drop onto the oversize table. "What's happened? Is Kristi okay? Is it your father? Is he all right?"

Renzo folded his arms like he'd done that very first day, and there was nothing of the gentle look he'd offered the past few weeks. He looked straight at her. "You had your lawyer call the judge today." Accusation deepened his tone. "You wanted to make sure she knew about Dad's health issues before she made a decision, even though you know what we've been going through with Dad. You know how dicey the situation is, and yet you still made that phone call. A phone call meant to change everything."

The grim look on his face cut straight to her heart, but it also toughened her backbone because didn't a just man offer benefit of the doubt? Or at least pose the question nicely? "It wasn't meant to do any such thing," she began, but he shook his head firmly and didn't let her speak.

"I trusted you. I believed you when you said you wanted to work out some kind of agreement, Sarah, but you went ahead and kicked us when we were down. And I don't know how something like that can be forgiven."

Forgiven?

His choice of words spiked old anger. "I don't believe I was asking for your forgiveness, was I?" She faced him, making sure she looked cool as a cucumber while her wretched heart melted inside. "Yes, I called my lawyer and asked him to make the judge aware of circumstances. He wanted to do it weeks ago and I said no. I wanted to give it time, and I did. I didn't have him call the judge today because I wanted to snatch the girls away or hurt you or your parents. I did it because it was the right thing to do because it's been weeks since your father got ill. I'm sorry you can't accept that."

"Accept it?" He stared at her, then scrubbed a hand across the back of his head. "Please go. I have enough to deal with today with a sick child and a very busy schedule. That's enough on anyone's plate."

Sarah swallowed hard. She took a step forward. "Renzo…"

Face hard, he moved farther away from her deliberately.

So that's how it was going to be.

She turned away from the cheerful Christmas tree in the big family room. Away from the table full of party supplies for the girls' upcoming birthday celebration.

And away from the plate of amazing cookies she'd made that morning. "Can I say goodbye to the girls?"

He shook his head. "They've had enough to handle for one day. Kristi's illness, then being forgotten at school. No, you've done quite enough. I'll tell them you've left. And now—" he included her mother in his look "—good day."

Sarah opened her mouth to reply, but her mother had crossed the room. Gently she took Sarah's arm. "Come on, darling. We've done our time here. Now we'll leave it to the courts."

The courts.

That was exactly what she didn't want now that she knew Renzo and his family, but she'd heard the determination in Gina's voice that morning. Roy's illness wasn't going to stop Renzo's mother from pushing for the adoption.

She walked to her car.

"Are you all right to drive?" Her mother whispered the words so that Renzo wouldn't overhear from the doorway, but when she glanced that way, the outer doors were closed and the rugged sheriff's detective was nowhere in sight.

Her chest was tight. The lump in her throat didn't allow words, so she just nodded and climbed into the car. She drove back to the rented apartment.

They hadn't taken time to decorate the temporary home. Darkness yawned before her, a sharp contrast to the merry twinkle lights they'd strung at the Calloway ranch.

Her mother came up the steps and then, only then,

did she allow the tears to fall. But not for long because she'd no sooner gotten in the door of the subleased apartment than her phone rang and the NICU phone number flashed in her screen.

"Dr. Brown." She answered swiftly, because the NICU didn't make calls casually.

"Sarah, it's Felicity." Felicity Dillon was a NICU nurse manager and a good friend. "We need you back, ASAP. Drs. Roundhouse and Fettah have both come down with the flu and we can't be this low on staff, and you know when two go down, more are sure to follow. Can I ask you to cut your break short?"

Going back to work was like a gift from God right then, because she could focus her thoughts and efforts on saving other people's children and not dwell on hardship she may have caused three precious girls. "I'll leave now. I can be back in the city in three hours."

"Grab some sleep first," Felicity warned. "We're covered for tonight, and if this spreads, you might be staying for a while. I've got your coffee pods waiting."

Felicity made a great point. Sarah kept it short. "See you at six, then."

Her mother was tossing their belongings into their suitcases. She indicated the three small piles of presents they'd gotten for the girls' birthday. "Should we drop these off? Or take them with us?"

Sarah didn't want to think of what she was going to miss this weekend or next week. The birthday party, the little play, the Christmas Eve services. Right now she needed to compartmentalize emotions and refocus her brain. The girls were safe and sound. They were in good hands.

She lifted a pile of gifts and moved toward the stairs. "I don't think our presence is welcome at the ranch right now. Let's take them along. We can ship them back tomorrow."

"I'll take care of it." Lindsay helped get the cars packed, and when they were done, and the apartment key had been left on the table, she tugged Sarah into her arms. "You did nothing wrong," she whispered into Sarah's ear. "Nothing. And maybe Gina isn't as bad as she seems right now. With all that's gone on, I expect she's desperately trying to keep things going her way, but her plates are spinning out of control. Or maybe she's just wretched."

Her alternative reasoning almost made Sarah smile.

"Either way, the judge needed to know what was happening," Lindsay continued. "The lawyer said she was unaware of your existence or Roy's health struggles, and how can a judge make a good decision if half the facts are hidden?"

"I know you're right, and yet I still feel like a tattle-tale," Sarah said. She wouldn't mention that leaving the girls and Renzo was the hardest thing she'd ever done. She was still too angry to rationally deal with his abrupt about-face.

If he truly cared for her, wouldn't he have asked what happened? Or did he really think she deliberately went behind his back?

She'd never know now. His problem. Not hers. Except her broken heart didn't want to believe that.

Her mother gave her one last hug. "See you in the city."

"I've got this, Mom." She squared her shoulders and met her mother's look of concern. "I'm not even going to unpack the car once it's parked. I'm going to crash and get six hours of sleep and then show up at work for however long they need me. Babies await."

"I love you, Sarah." Lindsay hugged her fiercely one last time. "Drive safe."

"You, too."

They took I-90 toward the coast, and when the nearby exit for Golden Grove shone bright in her headlights, Sarah took a deep breath.

The few lights of the small town were gone quickly, but the cozy town with its rural appeal and lush farms and orchards hadn't just tugged her heart. It grabbed it, full force, because she wasn't just leaving the town. She was leaving people she loved, and the angry words and uncertain future left her feeling bereft.

But the image of Renzo's grim, determined face set her resolve.

Her heart longed to break.

She didn't let it. In a few hours she'd be caring for the tiniest of humans, giving it her all, and it was time to put their health and happiness first.

Chapter Thirteen

Sarah had double-crossed them. After nearly five weeks of being indispensable, she'd gone behind his back to inform the court of his father's health scare. She could have waited for the family to inform the court, but she didn't.

She took it upon herself, and that made the Calloways look devious. On top of that, he felt stupid. He wasn't used to being duped, and he wasn't the type that was generally snowballed by women. Until now, that was. This time he'd been ready to fall hook, line and sinker for the first time ever. Now she'd saved him the trouble.

He tried not to grumble around the girls, so when Naomi looked for Sarah, he worked to keep his tone level. "She had to leave."

"With her mom?" Naomi pressed.

"Yes. Do you want mac and cheese or buttered pasta for supper?" His attempt to change the subject didn't work.

Naomi climbed onto one of the counter-height seats

and frowned. "But we were going to make our treat bags for our birthday party."

"Treat bags?" He angled a look down as he added pasta to boiling water.

"You know, the little bag everybody gets when they go to a party. Auntie showed us some treats and sticky things and puzzles and everybody gets one. Can we make them now?"

He'd stowed the pile of shopping bags in the closet, figuring he'd deal with all that later. He shook his head. "Let's have supper first and watch over Kristi. She's still really sick."

"I wish she wasn't." Chloe dragged her feet as she came down the stairs. "I wanted to have Auntie figure out games for the party. She said she would."

"I know how to play games," he assured her, but her expression was filled with doubt.

"Not, like, outside games, cuz it's too cold and wet. Like the games at other kids' parties."

He had no idea what she was talking about, but he was nearly forty years old and kids' parties weren't exactly rocket science. One internet search and he'd be all set. "I'll figure it out. I promise."

"It's okay. Auntie will do it when she gets back," Naomi assured him, and his breath caught sideways in his chest. Should he tell them she wasn't coming back? At least until the judge issued a decision?

The girls' hopeful expression made him stay quiet, but by the next morning, Naomi wasn't about to let the topic fade. "I think we should call Auntie Sarah. Just to see. Like, maybe she's sick, Renzo." Worry formed that little furrow between her eyes, a furrow she'd had since birth. "Because she promised she'd help, right? And I don't think she misunderspoke."

The butchered word did him in. He sat down and faced her and Chloe at the big dining table. "Sarah won't be at your party."

Quick tears filled Naomi's eyes. She swiped at them, but her chin quivered and more tears spilled over. She tried to speak, but all that came out was a strangled sob.

"I knew she probally wasn't coming." Chloe's stress showed in the mispronunciation of a word she knew well. "Our mom left us a long time ago and now Auntie Sarah left us and she didn't even say goodbye." Her chin didn't quiver. It went tight and her lower lip stuck out when she folded those arms rigidly across her chest. "When you love somebody, you always say goodbye. Always."

Regret sucker punched Renzo. By standing his ground against Sarah's duplicity, he'd made a crucial mistake, because the girls needed closure. How was he going to fix this? He started to speak, but Chloe stomped up the stairs, and when she reached the top step, the little girl who rarely cried swiped both hands to her cheeks to wipe away tears. "Chloe…" He started to go after her, but Naomi put her head down on the table and sobbed, brokenhearted.

He'd blown it. He'd been so entrenched in his reaction that he hadn't thought about the girls' needs. Trying to protect them, he'd hurt them and that was 100 percent his fault.

Kyle texted him a few minutes later. I can't get to the barn early. Will be there around eleven.

The text came at the absolute wrong time. The girls were angry, Kristi was still sick and there was no one to watch them to leave him free to take a shift in the barn. Kyle didn't know that, but Renzo was tired of covering for his brother. I'm alone with the girls. Can't leave the house.

A blank stretch of time ensued before Kyle texted back. Be right over.

Good. It was high time his brother took responsibility for this partnership with their father. Renzo was meant to offer occasional help, not daily routine so Kyle could chill out somewhere. He saw his brother's truck pull in ten minutes later, and he was gone in ninety minutes. He didn't stop in. Didn't grab coffee. Mad, most likely.

Well, join the club, thought Renzo as he gave Kristi her midday dose of medicine.

The Bible was filled with stories about troubled brother relationships. He'd always shrugged them off as examples for other people.

Not anymore. His brother had been shirking his duty for too long, and if no one else would call him out about it, Renzo intended to at the first possible opportunity.

But first he had to figure out how to juggle three girls without a babysitter. Kristi couldn't take part in their play that evening, and he needed to get the other girls there while keeping a very disappointed Kristi at home.

He called Tug Moyer. "I need a favor," he told his long-time best friend. "Kristi is sick, the other girls have their preschool play tonight and I can't bring Kristi along."

"I'll take the girls over," Tug said instantly. "What time?"

"Six o'clock? The performance is at six thirty."

"Consider it done. Is Sarah sick, too? And her mother?"

He'd been silly to think Tug wouldn't sense a problem instantly. "It was time to circle the wagons."

Tug had the nerve to snort. "Circle the wagons against the incredibly beautiful, smart, funny and affectionate aunt that wants to be part of their lives? Of course. What a smart thing to do."

"You don't understand—" Renzo began, but Tug cut him off.

"You're talking to the guy who carried a truckload of guilt around after losing his wife. The guy who made some pretty stupid assumptions before realizing that God only gives thickheaded guys like us so many second chances. I saw the way you looked at Sarah on the Candlelighting Walk. And the way she looked back. Why would any sane man want to pursue that?" he asked rhetorically, then he sighed purposely. "I'll pick up the girls, but I kind of hoped you wouldn't be as dense as I was. Obviously, I was mistaken. See you tonight."

Right about then Renzo wished he'd used the landline phone so he could slam down the receiver, but the minute he realized that, he knew why he wanted to do it.

Tug was right.

He'd been falling in love with Sarah Brown. Enough

to accept the impossibility of the situation considering their current circumstances, and then he'd sent her packing because she did what she came to do. What she'd *told* him she was going to do. His reaction said more about him than it did about her.

Kristi was sound asleep when he helped the other girls get ready for their play.

Naomi dragged her feet when he asked her to change into the white sneakers they were supposed to wear for the angel choir. "I don't want to go. Not without my sister. Not without Auntie."

"Me, either. This is all stupid," grumbled Chloe. She tugged the sneakers on, but didn't pretend to like it. "I'm not even going to sing anything. If Kristi can't sing, then I won't sing."

"'Cept I promised Miss Mamie that we'd sing extra loud, remember?" Naomi's torn expression gut-stabbed him. "I think she'll be so sad if we don't sing. 'Cept that I don't want to sing, not even a little bit."

He'd created a conundrum, and when he tried to mentally blame it on Sarah's choice, his conscience wouldn't let him. He'd never even given her the chance to talk about it. To explain. He'd reacted—

Possibly overreacted, he admitted to himself grudgingly.

And here he was, with two reluctant performers. "Uncle Tug will be here to get you in five minutes. Can we please cooperate and get ready? We'll talk about the rest tomorrow."

"Why should we go when nobody will even come to see us?" Chloe whispered. "You won't be there. Mama

Gina and Papa are gone. Auntie Sarah went away without even saying goodbye. Grandpa's too sick." She lifted her narrow shoulders in a helpless motion, and Chloe was never helpless. "I will just miss everybody so much."

It was a major admission from his most stoic ward. He pulled her into a hug. Then Naomi, too. And when Tug came to the door, Renzo switched places with him. "I'll take the girls if you're okay staying with Kristi." Tug had two older kids, so he knew the ropes when it came to childcare.

"You'll come?" Chloe's look of surprise melted Renzo's heart. "For real?"

"I don't want to miss a chance to hear you guys sing," he told her. "And Tug will take good care of Kristi."

"So maybe we can sing really loud, just like if Kristi was there," said Naomi. She grabbed for his hand. "And then we can hurry back and tell her, okay?"

"Very okay." He bundled them into the car, and as he found a spot in the elementary school auditorium, the difference from the previous year loomed starkly.

Lanny had been healthy enough to come the year before. Gina and Roy had both been there. Kyle and Valerie had come. He'd been there, cheering for three blond-haired little lambs, wandering into a very special stable under a bright star.

Tonight he was the only one there for the girls. The stark contrast didn't just make him think.

It made him regret his overdone reaction to Sarah the day before.

He looked around.

Was she here? Watching? He couldn't exactly ban her from being in a public place, and if she did come, the girls would be ecstatic.

He surveyed the entire small auditorium.

No Sarah.

Disappointment skewered him. Was she really going to miss this?

Well, you did throw her out of the house. She is possibly feeling quite unwelcome at the moment and wouldn't want a scene to mess with the girls' happiness.

He'd hurt her. Worse, he'd done it on purpose. His mother had been so upset when she called to report what their lawyer had shared, and his mother couldn't afford to be upset right now.

Piano music started. The lights dimmed. For the next thirty minutes, he watched an adorable play about lost angels, taking every wrong turn possible until eventually ending up right where they were supposed to be. At a Bethlehem stable, where a baby lay sleeping in a hay-filled manger.

The girls sang, as promised, but he couldn't fully grasp the simple joy of their performance because he'd messed up, and right now he saw no way to make this right. Not with so much on the line.

Sarah eyed a coffee pod, decided it was a stupid move if she could catch a nap later, and tried not to think about what she was missing in Golden Grove this weekend.

Was Kristi getting better?

Were the girls singing extra loud in the choir?

Had anyone else gotten sick?

Her mother texted her. Sent packages off to the ranch. Delivery tomorrow. In time for the birthday party.

Thank you!

She left it at that. Missing the girls' party was a heartbreaker, but maybe she'd be allowed to be part of the next one. And the one after that. She'd keep her eye on the true goal, to be part of their lives even if she wasn't awarded guardianship. She wouldn't think about Renzo...

Except she couldn't *stop* thinking about him, which was problematic.

But she'd *try* to stop thinking about him. He'd taken the big strong protector role too far. Except that if she wanted a big strong protector, the guy was absolutely number one in her book. But how dare he not let her say goodbye to the girls?

Well, you did tell the judge about his whole family crisis, didn't you?

She'd missed the play. The girls' party. And Christmas loomed, so she'd miss that, too, but as she worked to stabilize tiny infants in need of specialized care, she focused on her number one personal priority. She wanted the girls to be happy. To feel like they were loved and cherished. To feel like they belonged not just emotionally, but physically, and knowing they had a biological aunt who loved them would help that. If nothing else, the girls would always know they had an aunt, that she loved them and came to be part of their lives. If it didn't work out that way, they'd move forward knowing her choice was to love them.

"Dr. Fettah is coming back to work on Christmas Eve," Felicity told her Wednesday afternoon. "That means you get Christmas off."

She didn't need Christmas off. That day, of all days, she needed to keep busy and not dwell on all she'd lost in Washington's heartland. She could go to her parents' place on the island, sure. Then they'd all sit around, wondering how the girls were faring.

Or she could sit alone in her undecorated town house and watch the boats in the harbor. Another Christmas alone, but worse this time. Because this year she'd thought it would be different. "I need to work, Felicity. See if he'd like an extra day off."

"No can do," Felicity replied. "You've been on too long as it is, and you know the rules. Take the time and do something you really want to do, my friend. Get in your car and go see those girls. Even if it's just in church, you sitting on one side, them on the other. At least that way they won't think you've abandoned them, because I'm pretty sure that's what any child would think right now. No one can keep you out of a church on Christmas Eve, Sarah."

The possibility breathed hope back into her. "You think that's a good idea?"

Felicity shot her a wise look. "I know it is. Most likely, all the girls know is that you've disappeared. If you suddenly reappear, at least they know you still care. Honey, I've seen some ugly custody battles in my time.

Don't let this become one of them. Even if you have to go all King Solomon on them."

She sighed and nodded. "You're right. I hate that, but I can own it. I'll head inland on Christmas Eve and go to the service. At least that way I'm celebrating part of the day with them. And that means a lot."

"It means everything," Felicity promised.

Chapter Fourteen

Renzo drove to Seattle at the end of the week. His father had been cleared for transfer to the long-term care facility Lanny lived in. He'd shown some progress, but not enough to score a bed at the rehab center, but maybe he still could, given time.

Tug's mother came over to watch the girls while he made the long trek to the city to make sure everything went according to plan. At least his father would be closer to home, and that proximity might give him more reason to fight. If it didn't, at least he'd be housed nearby.

He walked into the hospital room. His mother and Shelly were busy gathering Roy's things into reusable shopping bags. He gave his grumpy-looking father a gentle hug and kissed him on the forehead. "Ready for the big move, Dad?"

Roy grunted. Grunting was his go-to response when he was unhappy with anything. The grunts used to be few and far between. Not anymore.

He'd gathered a handful of bags to take down to his car when Kyle walked in.

"I didn't know you wanted to come," said Renzo. "We could have driven together. That's a lot of wasted time and gas."

He could have scolded further. In fact, he was having a hard time keeping the floodgate of opinions at bay, but Kyle raised a hand to pause him. "I was already in the city."

Renzo didn't have to pretend surprise. "You were? Why?"

Valerie came through the door right then. Her red-rimmed eyes testified to her stress, but she slipped her hand into Kyle's and stood by his side. "Because of me," she said softly.

"Us," Kyle told her firmly, then he gave her a look of such love that Renzo felt it to his core. "I want to apologize to all of you," he went on. "I've been off my game mentally and physically, and I'm sorry about that. I realize now that I should have told you, that we were silly to keep this to ourselves. Now we want you to know."

"Know?" Gina slapped a hand to her heart. "Know what? What's going on? What's happening?"

"We've been going to the infertility treatment center," Kyle stated. He squeezed Valerie's hand lightly, then brought it up for a kiss. "We've been trying to start a family for years, and it's just not working."

"You never said a word." Gina looked from one to the other. "Why wouldn't you tell us?"

"I was embarrassed." Valerie breathed deeply. "I wanted a family so badly, and I've never been stymied by anything in my life, so when it didn't work, I was so angry and sad that I couldn't even talk about it. Eventually I couldn't bear to even come over to your place and see the girls. I was upset that you guys ended up with three beautiful children and I couldn't give my husband one. It seemed ridiculously unfair."

"But now we've come to a decision," Kyle told them, and for the first time in a long time he stood tall. "We're going to continue the treatments for another six months on the doctor's recommendation. But we're also going to put in an application for adoption. Seeing what a blessing the girls are, and how happy they've made you guys, we realized that maybe God's got a different plan for us. And maybe we were just too stubborn to see it."

"Oh, darlings." Gina surged forward and hugged both of them. "Whatever you decide is wonderful, but I'm brokenhearted that you've been going through this alone. I can call all my prayer partners, all my ladies leagues and the prayer warriors at Golden Grove Covenant and we'll—"

"Mom, you can pray. All of you. But this is part of why we kept it private," Kyle told her kindly. "We don't want everyone knowing. It's personal, all right? Valerie and I are private people."

"Although Sarah knows," Valerie said.

Renzo frowned. "Sarah knows?"

"I had a terrible day a few weeks back, and she's so amazingly understanding and smart and I just opened up to her."

"She never said a word."

"She promised she wouldn't," Valerie informed him,

"but she also promised to pray for us. She let me pour out my heart, and she just sat there and listened. And cried with me."

Empathy. Caring. Tenderness. And strength. Yeah, he'd noted all of those things in Sarah, then sent her away. What a dolt.

His mother could have used this opening to criticize Sarah. She didn't. In fact, she ignored Valerie's words altogether as a nurse came in with a wheelchair. "Ready to go?" the nurse asked.

"We are," Gina replied. "Renzo, can you call the home and reaffirm that they're expecting your father? I don't want any miscommunications to get in our way. The case manager's number is in my phone."

"Of course." He picked up her phone and scrolled for the home's number. Then he paused when a familiar number popped into view. A familiar number that came up as an outgoing call on a very important day. "Mom?"

She turned and looked at him.

He raised the phone. "You called Sarah on the same day her lawyer called the judge?"

The nurse had just handed Gina a sheaf of discharge papers. Two of the papers fluttered to the floor as her eyes went wide.

"You called her that morning?" he probed, because in all the discussions about the judge's notifications, this detail had never been brought up. "Why did you call her?"

Concern shadowed Aunt Shelly's face. She glanced from Gina to Renzo with a clear look of worry.

"To check on the girls, of course." Gina tried to brush

it off, but he'd been reading faces and actions for a lot of years. A woman who told the truth as a steadfast rule was fudging it today.

He shook his head. "You were still mad about the schedule changes, weren't you?" He glanced at the phone, then drew his attention back to her as the pieces fell into place. "They had just told you that they were going to transfer Dad to Westwood. You didn't like the doctors' decisions and you didn't want Sarah changing your influence with the girls and you snapped, didn't you?"

"I don't know what you're talking about. I don't snap." She glowered at him and motioned to his father. "And now is not the time to talk about this, with your father so ill."

On that she was correct, but the realization that she'd called Sarah that fateful morning spoke volumes. He held her gaze. He had a couple of choices here. To get all-out angry, have his say and stomp out, or option B.

Be nice. Because mom is actually a wonderful woman whose life had been turned upside down a few weeks back.

He chose the second option and gathered his over-anxious mother into a hug. A really good hug. "When did you stop trusting God?" he whispered into her ear. "Didn't you always teach us to trust His way? His path? And didn't He send Sarah to us at the best possible time?"

"I told her that very thing," Shelly declared. "But she let that silly pride get in the way. Of course stress will do that to you."

Renzo held on for a few more seconds, then released her. "The girls need her, Mom."

Kyle cleared his throat. Nice and loud. Loud enough for Renzo to add, "I do, too. So let's work this out. Not with courtrooms and lawyers. With love."

Valerie handed Gina several tissues as tears welled. Gina dried her eyes, blew her nose, then nodded. "You're right, of course. And I should have trusted your judgment from the beginning."

"I won't argue that," Renzo replied, then he rounded the bed and put an arm around his father's shoulders. "I love you, Dad. Let's get you back to Westwood. And if you do well there, I'll personally drive you over to the rehab center in Ellensburg. I can guarantee that they'd love to have you there. Their success stories are impressive."

Roy didn't grunt this time.

He looked up at Renzo, then at the rest of his family, and for the first time since the major stroke, he seemed agreeable. "Okay."

That single word might mean nothing, or a major turning point, but it was December 23 and Renzo had a lot to accomplish. The nurse ushered Roy out to the medical transport, and the Calloway family drove back to Golden Grove. But as soon as he got there, Renzo began laying out a new schedule. And this one involved three little girls, a long drive to the coast and Christmas in Seattle.

His only hope was that it wasn't too late.

Chapter Fifteen

Nerves thrummed along Sarah's spine for the entire drive to Golden Grove. She'd put gifts for the girls in the back, and she'd stocked her purse with chocolate and puffy peppermints, a favorite of all three girls. She might not get to give them the gifts or share the candy, but she'd be sharing the Christmas Eve service and that was the best thing of all.

The small church parking lot was full. The short street was full, too. Sarah found a spot in the municipal parking lot up the road. She pulled in, parked and hurried over to the church, just in time.

Sweet bells rang out clear notes to begin the service. An usher held the door for her, greeted her with a soft "Merry Christmas, miss!" and motioned her inside.

The service was standing room only, but that gave Sarah a clear vantage point. She scoured the church as the pastor began.

No Renzo.

No girls.

It wasn't a big church, and it was full, but even if she couldn't spot Renzo, it was hard not to notice identical triplets.

They weren't there.

Were they sick? Did she dare text and ask?

She tried to focus on the gentle prayers, but disappointment gripped her. She'd never thought of them not being here. This was the service they attended each year. Renzo and Gina had made that quite clear, and yet none of them were here today.

She climbed back into her car an hour later. The service had been poignantly beautiful, and the lilting notes of "Joy to the World" rang through the town as the bell tower played, but she'd driven hours to share this time of worship with her sister's children and that hadn't happened.

Sadness coursed through her.

She got into the car, and instead of heading back toward the coast, she drove to the ranch. She expected to see twinkle lights glowing merrily around the windows and draped from the porch. They'd set up Gina's outdoor Nativity scene, but on this night of all nights, the house stood dark and lonely. There were no lights, inside or out.

Something was wrong.

Her brain chided her swiftly. *Lots of people turn lights off when they're away. Don't borrow trouble.*

She wasn't borrowing trouble. She knew this family. Understood the importance of their customs. They liked tradition, so where were they? Had Roy taken a bad turn? Were the girls all right?

She raised her phone to text Renzo, but stopped herself at the last minute. Did she want to upset his Christmas? No.

She wanted answers, but it wouldn't be right to mess up whatever they'd planned with drama that could wait until after the holidays.

She took a deep breath, got back on the highway and started the loneliest drive she'd ever undertaken.

Normally, the exits off I-90 were bright with shops and services, but not at seven o'clock on Christmas Eve. Other than the occasional convenience store, everything was closed for the holiday.

The lights of the city brightened a dark skyline as she approached her exit, but they did nothing for the ache in her heart. She'd have preferred the twinkle-lit windows, and the miniature stockings framed in each pane, but that wasn't to be.

She parked the car, decided to leave the gifts right where they were and crossed the silent parking garage, half-empty because folks had gone away for the holidays.

She let herself into the building and walked down the narrow access hall to the lobby. The grand lobby tree blinked and winked colorful lights, but her heart wasn't tuned toward grandiose. It had been looking for a quieter, more rustic setting.

Chin down, she turned toward the bank of elevators.

"There she is!"

"It's Auntie!"

"Oh, Auntie Sarah, I've missed you so much! So much!"

Three little spitfires raced her way. She sank to her knees to hug each of them in turn, then all of them at once. "I can't believe you guys are here! I'm so excited to see you! All of you! And you're all better?" she asked Kristi quickly.

Kristi nodded. "I got all better, but then Chloe got sick and she was grumpy." She elongated the word on purpose. "And then Nomi got it, but she was just more sleepy and then we all got better and we came here to have Christmas with you!"

Renzo was standing across the lobby.

She raised her gaze to his.

He moved forward, almost reluctantly. "I know this is unexpected."

She stood, with the girls surrounding her. "That seems to be the way we do things."

His cheek quirked slightly. Almost a smile. "True. Sarah, I came to apologize." He moved closer, and the kind but troubled expression on his face tugged at her heart, but he hadn't exactly treated that heart with the tenderness it deserved, so she held back. "I was a jerk," he admitted in an apologetic voice.

Christmas or no Christmas, she wasn't about to disagree so she nodded while the girls leaped to his defense.

"You're not a jerk, Renzo," declared Chloe. "You're the best."

"You take really good care of us and you know how to fix Christmas lights," added Naomi. Her expression said that fixing Christmas lights was superhero-worthy.

"And you took such good care of all of us when we

were sick and Auntie couldn't be there," added Kristi. "But she's here now, and that makes this the best Christmas ever," Kristi went on. She gripped Sarah's hand. "This was my only dream," she whispered, but none of the girls were really good at whispering yet. "To have Christmas with all of us together. And Renzo made it come true!"

"But we were worried," added Naomi.

"Like a lot," cut in Chloe.

"Why?" Sarah asked.

"You weren't here," Naomi declared with a glance around the pretty lobby. "And we weren't sure where to go or what to do, and Renzo said if you didn't get home soon, we'd find a hotel or just sleep under the Christmas tree and you'd come home and find us all sleeping under the tree and you'd love us again."

Her heart crunched and she crouched to regather the girls into her arms. "I have never stopped loving you. Not for one minute of any day. I will always be your aunt and I will always love you. Every day. Every minute. I promise."

"But you didn't come hear us sing or anything." Chloe didn't waste time. "Even if you were mad at Renzo, you could have come and listened to us sing, right? Because that's what you do when you love somebody?"

Sarah sat right down on the floor and motioned to the girls to do the same. "I couldn't," she told them as the lobby manager crossed from his small office to the lobby desk. "I had to come back to work the night before the concert. Some doctors got sick. Really sick. And I take care of tiny babies, even tinier than you girls were when you were born, so they needed me to come back to work. Otherwise I would have been there, because that's exactly where I wanted to be. Maybe I can come next year, okay?"

Now she raised her gaze to Renzo. The look he gave her—consternation mixed with sweet affection—gripped her heart.

He reached for her hand.

She shouldn't take his hand because this man, this singular human being, couldn't just break her heart. He could crush it. Her fault for falling in love with a man of strength and resolve, the very qualities that drew her to him. He stood there, holding her gaze, hand outstretched, and there was no way she could resist. She took his hand. Let him help her up. And right then the lobby manager raised a jar of bright-toned candy canes for the girls to see. "Girls, would you like a candy cane?" he asked.

"We love these!" Chloe led the charge.

"They're the best, thanks, mister!" said Kristi.

"My favorite is cherry," breathed Naomi as she accepted a rose-toned candy cane. "Thank you! Is it okay if we eat them, Renzo?"

"Absolutely."

"I've got *The Grinch* playing in my office," the manager told Sarah and Renzo. "If you folks need a minute."

"That would be great," Sarah replied. "Thank you, Arthur." She turned back toward Renzo as the girls skipped into Arthur's office, then raised her gaze. "You came to the city."

A tiny smile softened his jawline. "We wanted to surprise you. I never considered that you might still be working."

"I wasn't," she admitted. She took a deep breath and let it out slowly. "I went to Golden Grove."

A brighter smile wiped the edge of worry from his eyes. "Did you, now?"

"On the advice of a dear friend, I realized that even if I couldn't spend time with the girls, I could pray with them. In the same church, at least. Then they weren't there, and your parents' house was all dark, and it was all wrong. So wrong."

"You went to the house?" He raised a hand to cradle her cheek. "Even though I was a total jerk, regardless of four-year-old opinions."

"And you drove here even though you were pretty sure I was out to ruin your family and your life. An absolutely incorrect assumption, by the way, and you never once gave me time to explain."

"Forgive me."

Two sweet words that meant so much.

"I found out the other day that my mother called you," he explained. "I knew she was mad about Dad's prognosis and she chewed me out about the change in scheduling, but I didn't realize how upset until I asked her about that phone call. She's sorry, too, but I'll let her apologize in person. If you don't mind giving us a second chance, Sarah."

She'd been given the gift of a peaceful, loving family as an infant. The girls should have the same. "It would be good for the girls if we all got along," she agreed, but then he surprised her once again when he slipped that hand behind her head and drew her into one of those amazing hugs she'd been missing.

"I agree. And while three hours isn't an unthinkable distance, it's real hard to get to know the most amazing woman who's ever walked into your life when you're both working crazy hours, you've got three kids who need constant attention and stuff keeps getting in the way. I propose we shorten the distance because there's nothing more important to me right now than having the chance to be with you." He paused and kissed the right side of her face. "Talk to you." He shifted his mouth to the opposite side and gently kissed that cheek. "Fall in love with you." This time he touched his lips to hers, and when he deepened the kiss, her heart caved completely. "I can't do that if I'm working on a case three hours away."

"And I can't move the hospital," she told him when they paused the kiss. "They need me here, in the city, where I can do the most good."

"I thought of that," he replied. He kept one arm snugged around her. He used the other hand to pull his phone from his belt loop and held up a picture. "That's my application to the Snohomish County Sheriff's Office. They called me the minute it showed up in their in-box. It's thirty minutes from the city. Less if we find a place closer."

She stared at the phone, then him. "You'd move here?"

"For you?" His face softened into the smile she'd come to know so well. The smile she'd missed since that fateful day. "In a heartbeat, Sarah. Of course, I'll need your advice," he teased when he paused kissing her again. "Shopping for a house. That's not exactly my expertise. And the girls will have to adjust, but when I balanced things out, being with you was more important than anything. To all four of us."

"Renzo, what about your parents?" Disbelief vied with joy. "They love these girls."

"They do. And my mother hates to have them so far away, but she weighed that up against my happiness in finding the most amazing woman in the world who happens to be the girls' aunt, and she not only gave me her blessing, she cried. But this time for joy, Sarah."

She couldn't believe it, and yet it was real. Wonderfully real.

"But we do have a current conundrum tonight," he told her. "I've got to find a place to stay with the girls, and I was scrolling while we were waiting for you. Shockingly—" he made a face to indicate it wasn't shocking at all "—all the hotels are full."

"All but one," she told him. She texted her mother quickly, and when Lindsay sent back a thumbs-up, she put away the phone. "Let's head to the island. We'll have Christmas at my parents' house. Mom's always got a stocked freezer, and the girls' gifts are in the trunk of my car. All we need now is three little girls, Renzo."

He gave her one last beautiful hug. "All we need now is us, darlin'. And we've got that. Let's transfer the gifts to my SUV. I've got some tucked there, too. I don't want to drive separate if we don't have to. Are you on call?"

"I'm off until eight o'clock tomorrow night."

"Perfect."

And it was. Far more than she had ever expected. They crossed the bridge with the girls singing carols in the back seat, and with Renzo, her love, behind the wheel. And it wouldn't matter if they ran out of eggnog or the cookies were a little stale or they had to add extra potatoes to make the small turkey stretch.

They were together as a family and that made it the best Christmas of all.

Epilogue

~❦~

"A summer wedding." Lindsay clipped the veil she'd worn at her wedding into the back of Sarah's hair and smiled at her reflection in the mirror. "A son-in-law I love, three beautiful granddaughters and the blessing of having you all living nearby. I couldn't ask for anything more." She hugged Sarah lightly. "You made our lives complete the day they put you into my arms, darling. And not one thing has changed since. We love you and we couldn't be more proud of you." She leaned down and kissed Sarah's cheek as a soft knock came at the door.

Her friend Felicity was the matron of honor. She moved to the door and drew it open. "Gina. Come in."

"It's all right?" Gina peeked around the door, saw Sarah and smiled. "I could not imagine a more wonderful bride for my son or a more perfect mother for those girls, Sarah." She crossed the room quickly and gave Sarah a light embrace. "Let me say just two things," she told them. "I was scared last year. You know that.

I was in danger of losing my husband and I thought in danger of losing the girls. I wasn't myself," she added. "I wasn't thinking right, because when I finally paused to talk to God, to give it up to Him, my eyes weren't just opened. They were opened to the joy it all brings. I know what the agency did was awful."

She gripped Sarah's hands and included Lindsay with a look. "But while it was awful, it also did an immense amount of good. You and Jenn brought great happiness to your parents. If Jenn hadn't been there, Lanny would have gone through life alone after losing his wife. There wouldn't be three beautiful girls all dressed in white, waiting to walk down the aisle. I would never have known the joy of them or you. I forgot to trust the plan," she admitted. "I like to run things, and when everything fell apart last November, it all spun out of control. But not now," she reaffirmed. "Now Valerie is expecting a Valentine's baby, my son is marrying a wonderful woman and the girls will be blessed with family. And I can devote my time to helping Roy continue his recovery. It all worked out perfectly, and we have you to thank for that. Because you never gave up. Even when my stubborn son and his equally stubborn mother got in your way." She held out a beautiful necklace that featured golden brown stones, unlike anything she'd ever seen before. "For you," Gina told her. "It was my mother's and she gave it to me. And now I want to pass it on to you."

"It's beautiful, Gina. Thank you."

Renzo's mother smiled. "Much like the bride, I'd say."

"You could wear it today," suggested Lindsay. "It goes beautifully with your eyes."

"It's stunning." Sarah touched Gina's arm gently. "Can you put it on me, please?"

"With pleasure."

Lindsay lifted the veil. Gina affixed the delicate chain, then stood back and smiled. The soft tones of a prelude began.

"It's time." Sarah's father, Kevin, came to the door. "They're waiting to escort two mothers down the aisle. And I'm waiting for one incredible daughter."

Lindsay and Gina hurried toward the center aisle. Sarah looped her arm through her father's and stretched up to kiss him on the cheek. "I figured out why I waited so long to fall in love," she told him.

"Yeah?" Kevin smiled. "Why's that?"

"Because it took me this long to find a man as wonderful as you."

Her father's eyes filled. He clutched her arm a little tighter. "I said no tears. Yours or mine. Save the sentimental stuff for later, all right?"

She laughed because it was more than all right.

As the notes of music signaled the mothers' entrance, three little loves dashed her way.

"Auntie, you look like the most beautiful person ever!" Wide-eyed, Kristi paused and clasped her hands together as if afraid to touch Sarah. "Better than a princess, even."

"And we look like you!" Naomi twirled in the full-skirted white flower girl gown. "Like we're all supposed to be together because we match! This is so very special, Auntie Sarah! I love it so much! And I love you so much!"

"Me, too," she told Naomi as she opened her arms to welcome them with a hug. "I love that we're all going to be family together."

Chloe had hung back slightly. She came forward for the hug, but when the music changed, indicating the girls turn to process, she reached for Sarah's hand and pressed a small envelope into it. "Grandpa wanted me to give this to you," she whispered. "He said to tell you he loves you and he's sorry he can't be here and he's so glad we found you."

Sarah looked down. Printed on the outside of the envelope were three small, shaky words. "Your mother's letter."

Funny.

She'd wondered about her mother, about the choices made for so long, and now—

It wasn't that it didn't matter.

It just didn't matter *as much* because they were all here together, as family. And that's what she had gone to Golden Grove to find.

She bent low to hug Chloe. "Thank you for being Grandpa's messenger, Chloe. I'll treasure this forever."

Chloe met her gaze. And then, with a gesture of unscripted love, she reached for Sarah's hand and gripped it tight. "I love you, Aunt Sarah. And I will always be happy that you never gave up on us, like ever, because that's kind of what a mom does, isn't it?" Three pairs of golden-hazel eyes sought hers as Chloe continued.

"They try to never, ever give up because they love you so much."

Oh, her heart. She reached out and hugged them one more time while she exchanged a watery look with her father. "That's exactly what moms do. And now there are three girls who better walk down the aisle, because it's time, darlings."

They scooted away and took their place in front of Felicity. The gathering of wedding guests made a soft collective gasp as they spotted the three girls coming their way.

"Our turn." Her father propped his arm for her to grab hold.

"It is." She smiled up at Kevin, then looked toward the altar where her love waited.

He'd been whispering something to Kyle. When he looked up—saw her—he stopped talking. For a few beautiful seconds it was just the two of them, in love, beginning not just a new chapter, but a whole new book.

And she couldn't ask for anything more.

* * * * *

Dear Reader,

I absolutely loved writing this book. I fell in love with Renzo in *Learning to Trust* and couldn't wait to tell his story. Setting it at Christmas just made a great story better, don't you think?

We've experienced both sides of adoption in my family. There have been babies given up and children brought in, so seeing this issue wasn't hard, but it is emotionally draining. What if Sarah and her sister Jenn had gone to one family? Would the other family ever have gotten a child to love?

As the popularity of DNA testing increases, more and more families are connecting with people they didn't know, and maybe didn't even know existed. Things have changed and we change with them, don't we?

Wishing you all a Merry Christmas and a healthy and happy New Year. God bless you! Email me at loganherne@gmail.com, visit my website ruthloganherne.com and friend me on Facebook! You can also find me serving up food in the Yankee Belle Café every Thursday, or with a great group of folks in Seekerville!

And thank you so much for making this beautiful Christmas story part of your holiday season!

Ruthy

 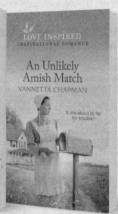

SPECIAL EXCERPT FROM

LOVE INSPIRED
INSPIRATIONAL ROMANCE

*When Mennonite midwife Beth Ann Overholt went to
Evergreen Corners to help rebuild after a flood, she
never expected to take in three abandoned children—
especially with an Amish bachelor by her side. But this
temporary family with Robert Yoder might just turn out
to be the perfect Christmas gift...*

Read on for a sneak preview of
An Amish Holiday Family
by Jo Ann Brown,
available November 2020 from Love Inspired!

"You don't ever complain. You take care of someone
else's *kinder* without hesitation, and you're giving them a
home they haven't had in who knows how long."

"Trust me. There was plenty of hesitation on my part."

"I do trust you."

Beth Ann's breath caught at the undercurrent of
emotion in his simple answer. "I'm glad to hear that. I got
a message from their social worker this afternoon. She
was supposed to come tomorrow, which is why I stayed
home today to make sure everything was as perfect as
possible before her visit."

"I wondered why you didn't come to the project house
today."

"That's why, but now her visit is going to be the day after tomorrow. What if she decides to take the children and place them in other homes? What if they can't be together?"

Robert paused and faced her. "Why are you looking for trouble? God brought you to the *kinder*. He knows what lies before them and before you. Trust *Him*."

"I try to." She gave him a wry grin. "It's just…just…"

"They've become important to you?"

She nodded, not trusting her voice to speak. The idea of the three youngsters being separated in the foster care system frightened her, because she wasn't sure what they might do to get back together.

"Don't forget," Robert murmured, "as important as they are to you, they're even more important to God." His smile returned. "How about getting some Christmas pie before we have to fish three *kinder* out of the brook?"

With a yelp, she rushed forward to keep Crystal from hoisting Tommy to see over the rail. Robert was right. She needed to enjoy the children while she could.

Don't miss
An Amish Holiday Family *by Jo Ann Brown,*
available November 2020 wherever
Love Inspired books and ebooks are sold.

LoveInspired.com

Get 4 FREE REWARDS!

We'll send you 2 FREE Books plus 2 FREE Mystery Gifts.

Love Inspired books feature uplifting stories where faith helps guide you through life's challenges and discover the promise of a new beginning.

FREE Value Over $20